PRAISE FOR WOLF HAAS
AND *BRENNER AND GOD*

"*Brenner and God* is one of the cleverest—and most thoroughly enjoyable—mysteries that I've read in a long time. Wolf Haas is the real deal, and his arrival on the American book scene is long overdue." **—CARL HIAASEN, AUTHOR OF *SICK PUPPY***

"Simon Brenner, the hero of Wolf Haas' marvelous series of crime thrillers, is a wildly likable and original character—a delightful and unexpected hero to show up in this noble and enduring genre. That Brenner struggles his way—always humanistically, often humorously—through Haas' acutely suspenseful narratives without the aid of a firearm, armed only with his smarts and sometimes fallible intuition, is a monumental plus." **—JONATHAN DEMME, OSCAR-WINNING DIRECTOR OF *THE SILENCE OF THE LAMBS***

"A must for crime fiction lovers with a sense of humor: In Simon Brenner, Wolf Haas has created a protagonist so real and believable that I sometimes wanted to tap him on the shoulder and point him in the right direction!" **—ANDREY KURKOV, AUTHOR OF *DEATH AND THE PENGUIN***

"Drolly told by an unidentified yet surprisingly reliable narrator, *Brenner and God* is very funny, leavened throughout with a finely honed sense of the absurd." **—LISA BRACKMANN, *NEW YORK TIMES* BESTSELLING AUTHOR OF *ROCK PAPER TIGER* AND *GETAWAY***

"This quirkily funny kidnapping caper marks the first appearance in English of underdog sleuth Simon Brenner.... Austrian author Haas brings a wry sense of humor.... American readers will look forward to seeing more of Herr Simon." **—*PUBLISHERS WEEKLY***

"The reader gets a double benefit: a story that is engaging and has a rapid momentum and a narrative voice that is darkly comic... My long wait for the Brenner books was delightfully fulfilled."

—*INTERNATIONAL NOIR FICTION*

"From the insanely talented and clever Wolf Haas... A satirical and cynical criticism of Austrian and German society is very much a part of the plot, just as Chandler, Hammett and the other great American hard-boiled writers had an indictment of our society at heart."

—*THE DIRTY LOWDOWN*

"One of Germany's most loved thriller writers: he's celebrated by the literary critics and venerated by the readers." —*DER SPIEGEL*

"This is great art, great fun." —*GERMANY RADIO*

"He is highly entertaining... It's as if he sits on Mount Everest looking down at other thriller writers." —*FRANKFURTER RUNDSCHAU*

THE BONE MAN

WOLF HAAS

THE BONE MAN

TRANSLATED BY ANNIE JANUSCH

 MELVILLE HOUSE
BROOKLYN · LONDON MELVILLE
INTERNATIONAL
CRIME

THE BONE MAN

Originally published in German as *Der Knochenmann* by Wolf Haas

© 1997 Rowohlt Taschenbuch Verlag, Hamburg

Translation © 2012 Annie Janusch

Lyrics on pages 86–87 are from "Die Alten Rittersleut," by Kurt Valentin

First Melville House printing: February 2013

Melville House Publishing
145 Plymouth Street
Brooklyn, NY 11201

www.mhpbooks.com

ISBN: 978-1-61219-169-0

Manufactured in the United States of America
1 2 3 4 5 6 7 8 9 10

A catalog record for this book is available from the Library of Congress.

CHAPTER 1

Well, something's happened again.

Spring's a glorious time of year, though—poems and all that. And everybody knows, it's in springtime that life awakens. That's why nobody wanted to believe it at first when suddenly it was the other way around.

Times change, though. What we would've given in the end if it'd only been as bad as it'd looked in the beginning. And that was only three weeks later—still spring. And then the summer—ruined by rain, you can forget about July—but a first-rate spring.

And if you'd seen Brenner sitting there at the Löschen-kohl Grill, you would've been hard-pressed to guess what had dragged him down there. You might've even mistaken him for a day-tripper, taking advantage of the spring day for a jaunt into East Styria.

And it would've been wiser for him to take a day-trip through Styria's sleepy vineyard towns. Enjoy the countryside a little, taste a little wine, eat a little fried chicken—and suddenly you're feeling like all's just a little bit well in the world still.

Never in all my days will I understand how a thing like that could happen in a place like this.

The spring wields such power, though—a person can't not

feel nature. And you could be wading knee-deep in blood when, all of a sudden, it's love you're thinking about. Now, Brenner may have been at the Löschenkohl Grill waiting for his food, but in his thoughts he was someplace else entirely. He was checking how long it'd been since his fiancée had run off. Believe it or not: twelve and a half years.

It wasn't just spring that had him thinking like this, though. No, whenever Brenner ate fried chicken, he'd automatically think of Fini. Her name was actually Josefine—needless to say, everyone called her Fini.

And you'd be hard pressed to find a person who liked to eat fried chicken as much as Fini did. Because she'd eat two, three chickens every week—practically addicted. And to watch Fini gnaw the bones clean, that was a real pleasure. Cannibals, no match. So, when Brenner walked into Löschenkohl's dining room, Fini came to mind, of course. Because Löschenkohl's is the kind of chicken place that—if you can imagine a furniture showroom or those garages where they park the jumbo jets. And the entire airplane garage is full of people eating fried chicken.

But then Brenner got interrupted and couldn't give Fini another thought. And besides, he shouldn't have been thinking about her for all that long anyway, because one thing you can't forget: only engaged two weeks. And so there wasn't all that much for him to remember, except for her incessant chicken-eating, and her huge rack, of course. Fini had said it was on account of the chickens being fed so many hormones.

But enough about Fini, because old man Löschenkohl himself was bringing Brenner his fried chicken, and you're going to be wondering why old man Löschenkohl would personally serve Brenner his fried chicken. Pay attention, though, because this is interesting: Löschenkohl offers his hand to Brenner and says: "Löschenkohl."

And Brenner lifts his rear half a millimeter off the wooden bench and says: "Brenner."

Old man Löschenkohl took a seat at Brenner's table. But these days, of course, when two people are sitting together and each is waiting for the other to say something, well, conversation's a little tricky.

"Dig in," Löschenkohl went on, and then they sat next to each other in silence until Brenner had finished the first piece of chicken.

And one thing you can't forget. There are four pieces in a Löschenkohl chicken, and even if you eat just two of them, you're going to bust a gut. That's why when you ask for the check, the waitress automatically brings you some aluminum foil, so that later on at home you've got yourself a decent snack, which is why Löschenkohl's is known throughout Styria—well, until you get to Graz. Even the Viennese come down on the weekends when they don't know how to fill up their greedy children anymore.

So, you've got Brenner with his half a chicken and his beer, and by contrast old man Löschenkohl with his wee glass of Löschenkohl's house wine—because he's got his own vineyard out back behind the place. And Brenner's just waiting to see if old man Löschenkohl doesn't have something to say for himself now.

But old man Löschenkohl didn't say a word and just silently watched his guest pick the bones clean. The old man's cheeks had turned purple—you could count every last vein—and he breathed about as heavily as an old mail truck. When Brenner had finished the first piece and placed the bones in the bone dish, his host asked: "What do you think?"

Now, did he mean the chicken, or did he mean would Brenner take the job? Because it was the kind of job, of course, that you have to think about three times before you take it. But Brenner couldn't say yes one way or another because the chicken was covered in a batter that was a centimeter thick and tasted like any number of things, just not like chicken.

"No wonder you're famous throughout these parts," Brenner said.

"A little less famous wouldn't hurt."

Löschenkohl was so tall that even seated he was still half a head taller than Brenner. There are so many tall people nowadays, and it wasn't unusual for Brenner to have to look up to the younger folks. People didn't used to be this tall, though. And now Brenner was reminded of how, when he was in the police academy, they took a field trip once to a castle—everything magnificent, but the lord's bed had been no larger than a child's.

Maybe it only occurred to him now because old man Löschenkohl had a certain something about him—I don't want to say "regal," but a dignified old chicken king, sure.

"Why do you want to stir up old history?" Brenner said, even though one really shouldn't speak with one's mouth full.

"We want the matter cleared up once and for all."

"But business is still good?"

"Business, yes."

"How many chickens do you sell in a week?"

"Ten thousand in a good week, five thousand in a bad week."

"And so you've got a problem with the bones?"

"No, no. We don't have a problem with them anymore."

"But you did."

"Back then, sure. By the time it became an issue, we had a problem with the bones. We paid the price, though."

"How many bones is that, then, with ten thousand chickens?"

"Mm, let's say forty percent bones. Let's say: four tons in a good week."

"So, almost a ton a day."

"In a good week."

"And so the bones got out of hand?"

"Back then they did. The business grew too quickly—each year we had to expand to keep from getting devoured by taxes. Needless to say, the bones got out of hand."

"And now?"

"We've had a new bone-grinder in the basement for some time now. It's not a problem anymore."

"But you had a bone-grinder back then, too?"

"Yes, but it was much too small. Because while the business might've grown and grown, the bone-grinder didn't grow with it."

Brenner was having a tougher time with his breaded chicken breast now, because the fat had started to run—not for vegetarians, let it be said.

"And who was working the bone-grinder back then?"

"The Yugo."

"And it was the Yugo who noticed the bigger bones mixed in with the chicken bones?"

"No, no, the Yugo didn't notice anything. Because we don't

just do chicken. We have all sorts of things. A ham hock's just as big, so the Yugo didn't notice anything."

"So who noticed it, then?"

"Well, the health inspectors came. Because we couldn't keep up with the bones anymore. Every day we were getting more and more customers, and every day more bones, of course, and every day the Yugo fell farther behind on the bone-grinding. Now, of course, so that it doesn't stink as much, we keep the bones in the walk-in freezer. Needless to say, the health inspectors went into the freezer."

"So they were the ones who made the discovery?"

"What do you mean, 'discovery'? Once you let the health inspectors in, they're always going to find something. They make you think you're some kind of criminal just because you own a chicken joint."

Brenner launched into the breaded drumstick, because when the owner's sitting at your table, you can't very well leave half a chicken on your plate.

"Grill," the old man corrected himself. "We've got everything, pork and so on. Ninety percent chicken, of course. But all that about the chicken bones didn't have to become such a big deal. We went and bought the Yugo a new bone-grinder—a modern one, ten times the capacity, and the Yugo only has to push a button, that's it. Pick it up with your hand."

Now, that would be referring to Brenner's chicken. Because Löschenkohl saw that he was cutting painstakingly around the chicken bones.

"A real poultry eater uses his hands," old man Löschenkohl said. But Brenner wasn't much of a poultry eater, per se, and he would have preferred to eat the greasy chicken leg off the plate.

His host wasn't having it, though: "Even in the finest establishments you're allowed to eat a chicken with your hands."

Before the old man could go any further, Brenner picked up the chicken and said: "And then what?"

"Then, the matter with the human bones, of course."

"That's what the health inspectors filed a complaint about?"

"What do you mean, 'health inspectors'? The police were called in immediately."

"Mhm."

"Whoever did it wasn't stupid, mixing the body in with our bone pile. Because, just between the two of us, it was more like Bone Mountain back then, what with the Yugo only having the small grinder."

"But it was found out nonetheless."

"Nothing's been found out, nothing at all. To this day, the police haven't found anything. Not even who the bones belonged to. The health inspectors, they're competent, they'll always find something. But the police, they didn't find half of what the health inspectors did."

With every bite now the chicken was tasting better and better to Brenner. Required some getting used to at first, but then, nice and crispy, that's the main thing. Because Brenner wasn't exactly a gourmand, either. But then, in the middle of the drumstick, he simply had to give up. And the third and fourth pieces—don't even think about it.

"What, you don't like it?" the old man asked, hurt. But you could tell right away that it was only mock-hurt. Because, these days, when a restaurateur has portions so big that his guests can't finish them, needless to say, he's proud.

"Too much," Brenner gasped.

WOLF HAAS

"I won't bring you any aluminum foil. You'll get a fresh one this evening," old man Löschenkohl said. "You're staying with us, of course."

Now, this was going a little too fast for Brenner. He hadn't even met the manager yet, who'd called him so desperately the day before.

"I'll need to speak with the manager first."

"With the manager?" Löschenkohl asked, as if he'd never heard of a manager before.

"She's the one who called me."

"Ah, my daughter-in-law, you mean. Yes, you'll be needing to talk with her, too. I'll go get her for you."

The old man stood up and took Brenner's half-finished plate with him to the kitchen.

But the manager wasn't there just then.

CHAPTER 2

You can wake Brenner up in the middle of the night and ask him who won the 1976 Olympic Downhill, and he'll know. Because that was his first year on the police force, and on the day of the Olympic Downhill, he had to break into a hotel staffer's room. There was a street-level lobby that took you from the main road that runs through the town of Hallein directly to the staffer's room. More like a laundry room, where the waiter from the Kino Bar had been put up.

A few people were standing in front of an electronics store on the other side of the street because the Olympic Downhill event was being broadcast on the color TV screens in the window display. And maybe that's why Brenner and his colleague didn't get the door open for so long, because they kept looking over at the Olympic coverage.

Even now, Brenner could still remember how his colleague had once torn his uniform jacket on a piece of sheet metal. Then, a few years later, he ordered a Filipina from a catalog who only weighed forty kilos. Brenner didn't know his name anymore. But the stench that they were met with when they finally got the door open—never in his life would he forget that. Even though the waiter from the Kino Bar had only been dead two days. And outside, people were celebrating, because the Austrian had finished with the best time, unbelievable, how a couple of people can make that kind of commotion.

But as old man Löschenkohl held the door open to Brenner's room in the staff's quarters above the restaurant, believe it or not, Brenner was struck by the exact same bestial stench. *Maybe it'd been the musty socks and sweaty waiter's shirts back in Hallein, and less so the decomposing*, Brenner thought, and threw open the window.

As he craned his neck out the window, he heard a squealing sound like a cement mixer, so loud that he whipped right back around and said to old man Löschenkohl: "That walk-in freezer of yours makes quite a racket."

"The freezer's on the other side of the house, in the addition. The most state-of-the-art walk-in freezer in all of Styria. Million-dollar investment. The interest on it just about eats me up. But you won't hear a peep out of it, because the whole thing's a computer, amazing."

Brenner didn't say anything to this, which made it all the easier to hear the squealing.

"What you're hearing is the bone-grinder. You're apt to hear it a bit. But what's worse are the birds in the morning."

"I believe it."

"Now that it's spring they're making an awful racket. That's something I can't do anything about. But if you'll be needing anything else," Löschenkohl said.

"No, I don't need anything."

Brenner was glad when the old man finally disappeared. He positioned himself at the window and took a moment to think in peace. He had two options. Either window closed and the stench. Or window open and the piercing squeal of the bone-grinder.

Or a third possibility, of course—up and out of there.

These days, though, if you want to skip out, you've got to do it right away. On the spot immediately. Because habit is a dog, and the next day something will come up, and the day after that you've already gotten a little used to it. And Brenner knew all about that. But the chicken had settled so heavily in his stomach that he decided: *I'll take a walk to digest.* And, of course, the walk calmed him right back down.

Maybe it was the warmth of the springtime sun, or maybe the idyllic country road, where a car would only drive by every five minutes. Or maybe it was just the green hills, because green's supposed to soothe the nerves, or so it's said. Maybe in the precincts where the police have green uniforms, the officers are less aggressive than in the places where they have other uniforms. And the people are more peaceable when they have green police officers. Whether the police suffer less abuse, you see—now, that'd be interesting.

Brenner couldn't have cared less. He hadn't worn a uniform in fifteen years. And it'd been a year since he'd even been a cop at all. So, he's walking through the Styrian vineyards now and thinking to himself: *here's a place where you can really walk, and what would be the harm if I were to stay a few days.*

It wasn't quite as isolated as it had first seemed. Because he'd been hearing some kind of din for the longest time now. At first he thought: *imagination.* Because it sounded almost like there was a soccer stadium just beyond the hills of the vineyard, like a hurricane of thousands of sports fans. And what can I say, beyond the hills there truly was a soccer stadium, and indeed, a few thousand spectators on wooden bleachers—so many that you might think they'd collapse any second now, and the entire town of Klöch, wiped out in an instant.

It was only when Brenner read the poster by the ticket stand that he understood how a team from a backwater like Klöch could have so many fans.

Because, needless to say, a Cup's a Cup. And the team from Klöch had drawn a Division II team from Oberwart—and Klöch usually plays five classes lower. So the Cup's the big chance for the little ones, every minor-league team believes it—today we're going to toss Goliath right out of that Cup. Practically biblical wrath.

Now, these games tend to be a little on the brutal side, of course. Because when the little ones catch a whiff of a chance, well, no telling what they'll do. This applies not just to soccer. It's often true for small countries, too, that they enjoy getting a little bloodthirsty if the opportunity's convenient. Now, I don't mean Austrians specifically—more of a general consideration.

And the Klöch soccer field was a bit of a madhouse now, because, right before the end of the game—and just as Brenner got there—still zero to zero. Two, three Klöch players were lying on the grass with leg cramps because—way out of their league, of course. Up, up and the game's back on! And the stars of the Oberwart team, one shot after another at Klöch's goal. But the goalkeeper—you wouldn't believe it. I'll just say: magician. And even that's an understatement.

Then, a foul called on a Klöch defender—and you could just hear the bones cracking. When the referee suspended the Klöch defender, the crowd was about ready to hang the ref. But police on the ground—thank god, you've got to admit—and the dog handlers were immediately deployed. The crowd was scared shitless by the sight of the German shepherds—and so the referee wouldn't be hanged after all.

After the extra time, the score still stood at zero to zero. So, needless to say, penalty kicks. The Oberwart team had a former striker from the national team playing for them, so he took the first penalty kick, of course. Right at the crossbar. Doesn't get more beautiful than that. But Klöch's goalkeeper—even more beautiful—he swatted the ball right out.

Why should I draw it out? The Klöch underdogs converted every penalty kick and threw Oberwart out of the Cup. Needless to say, a euphoria like that is infectious. And so it was that Brenner found himself in a completely different mood on the way home than he'd been on the way there. And you'd like to think that a person digests better under euphoric conditions. But when he arrived back at Löschenkohl's around seven, the chicken was still lodged in Brenner's stomach and he didn't have an appetite.

Nevertheless, Brenner went into the bar. Not because he wanted something to eat but because he thought, *it's about time I met the manager*. On the phone yesterday she'd been in such a hurry—she'd nearly started crying before Brenner promised her he'd come. And now she was making herself scarce. *But that's how managers are*, Brenner thought, *it's the same the world over*.

It was peak business in the dining room just now—Friday night, a dreadful horde of people dining out. *I don't want to bother the manager if she's working*, Brenner thought, and he took a seat at a table with a few drunken soccer fans because there was nowhere else to sit.

"Fried chicken?"

It was the same waitress as earlier that afternoon. She recognized Brenner right away and took his order ahead of the others who'd been waiting much longer.

"No, thanks," Brenner said.

"Or a pork knuckle? We've got good pork knuckles."

"For god's sake, no."

"Or spare ribs with french fries?"

"Just a beer," Brenner said, and he must have looked pitiful because the waitress gave him an encouraging look and then brought him his beer right away—before she even took the others' orders. She was wearing a red leather skirt, tight as a sausage casing. But, *the epitome of friendliness*, Brenner thought, and downed half his beer on the spot.

By about nine, business had slowed down, and as the waitress placed his third beer in front of him, Brenner asked her, "Is the manager around?"

"I haven't seen the manager at all today."

"When does she come in, then?"

"She must've already been in."

But the manager didn't show up after his third beer, either, so he ended up eating a schnitzel. No appetite at all, but Brenner's the kind of person who can't go to sleep unless he's had dinner. Sheer force of habit, but that's people for you. For every person who can't sleep on a full stomach, there's another who can't sleep unless it's on a full stomach.

So, down the hatch with the schnitzel, and another beer, too, and by ten Brenner was already back upstairs in the staff's quarters, lying in his bed. Or maybe hammock would be a better word for it. But he was so tired now that nothing could've disturbed him, not even the incessant squeal of the bone-grinder.

And let's be honest, people make an unbelievable fuss about sleep these days. It's got to be the best bed, everything organic, and absolute quiet, of course—the room gone through with a divining rod to see that the plumbing's rerouted whole-sale—just because people need to park their asses somewhere. Needless to say, no one could've dreamed of how soundly Brenner was sleeping tonight, what with half the Grill in his stomach.

But the deeper you sleep, the harder it is to wake up. That's the other side to this story.

When the waitress cleared Brenner's breakfast dishes the next morning, he had drunk his black coffee, but the rest he'd left. Butter and jam, all sealed up in their plastic capsules like you get everywhere today—might as well be landing on the moon. But it wasn't the shrink-wrapped portions that bothered Brenner. No, he was just a grouch in the morning—the very model of one, in fact.

The waitress, on the other hand, radiated an unusual cheerfulness: "Didn't touch anything, eh? Would you have preferred cheese?"

"No, no, it's fine."

"Or cold cuts?

"Cold cuts?"

"Assorted sliced meats."

Brenner knew what cold cuts were, of course. But the very word reminded him of the bones, i.e. the whole story of why he was sitting here at all, and grumpily, he asked the waitress: "What's with the manager?"

"What do you mean, 'what's with the manager'?"

"Where is she?"

"The manager? She hasn't come in yet." The waitress smiled and tiptoed back to the kitchen with the breakfast dishes.

It would've been fine by Brenner to just read the newspaper in peace. Because it's always interesting to read the local news when you're in a new place—because you get to read about problems that don't concern you at all. And to be perfectly frank, there's nothing more relaxing than that. Klöch's victory in the Cup took up half the paper. And on the front page, a photo of the goalkeeper being paraded like royalty around the field. More than 3,500 spectators had been in attendance—and that's in a town of only a thousand inhabitants.

There wasn't much else interesting in the paper, so Brenner was deliberating: *should I do the crossword puzzle now?* Because that had been a habit ever since his days as a traffic cop. A cop was often happy to work the night shift if it meant he could do the crossword.

But it's not without its perils, either, doing a crossword like that. A colleague of Brenner's got caught once after he'd completed an entire crossword puzzle book in one night. Not what you're thinking, though, he was just that good at crosswords. No, he'd written the same word over and over again. Namely: "depressed." What with the horizontal and vertical lines, though, it didn't always work out so well. Needless to say, early retirement at thirty-two. But, you see, you'd like to think the kind of danger that a cop has to face involves a shot getting fired or a car chase. You forget about the crossword, though.

Now, I wouldn't go so far as to say that Brenner was an

24

intuitive person. At work, he'd often wished he was: gut-feeling, and voilà, your perpetrator. But that wasn't one of his talents. Just like he wasn't particularly musical. Not especially gifted with languages, either. And even less so with math. He instinctively had no outstanding talent. If it's true, why shouldn't a man admit it? But, for once, his instincts were telling him something, and he did not solve the crossword.

Instead, he just watched the waitress roll the silverware into napkins and marveled at how anyone could be so cheerful at this hour of the morning. And men are all a little, you know, with things like this—let's be perfectly honest here. And so, naturally Brenner was thinking: *the waitress must've found herself a good lover to be that cheerful.*

One thing you can't forget, though. The waitress's room was immediately adjacent to Brenner's, and only some thin wood paneling in between. Because it used to be the attic, but at some point, they decided to spare every expense in dividing it up into lodging for their employees. Now, Brenner had slept so deeply through the night that he hadn't been woken up just before midnight by the waitress's lusty cries. But even asleep, you still hear it somehow. Unconsciously. And personally, I think that's why the lover occurred to him while he watched her bundle the silverware into the napkins.

Interesting, though! These days, if you watch a cheerful person, you'll feel cheerful, too. Well, maybe not cheerful, exactly, but all the same—Brenner was thinking to himself now: *who knows, maybe it's a good thing that the manager isn't here yet. I'll just take a look at the bone-grinder in the basement and have a little chat with the Yugo.*

That Brenner would go down to the basement: not exactly

remarkable. Because the bathrooms were also in the base-ment—enormous facilities, like at an airport. Because so much gets eaten there that, of course, you need a complementary latrine. And I've got to say, everything at Löschenkohl's: tip-top.

He bypassed the airport bathrooms and followed the squeal of the bone-grinder. It was an endless corridor, and the squealing grew steadily louder. And then he came upon a door. And when he opened the door—my dear swan! Brenner's morning coffee nearly came back up.

His first glimpse of the Yugo was a wide shot from behind. He was standing up to his hips in a pile of bones, feeding them into a machine that was nearly as long as all fifteen stalls in the men's bathroom. And the sheer smell of it. If you can imagine adding up all fifteen men's toilets here, too.

But the Yugo must have felt a draft from the door being opened. And as the Yugo turned around, wringing a couple of chicken carcasses in hands the size of dinner plates, Brenner instantly recognized him as the hero of the penalty shootout.

"You were in tremendous form yesterday," Brenner said. Because he was of the opinion that if you don't speak formal German with foreigners, they'll never learn the language.

"Sorry?"

"Yesterday. Tremendous form!"

"Sorry, my German. Sorry."

"Congratulations! Oberwart, no goal, you!" Brenner said, and you see how quickly a good intention can crumble. Some-times, though, success gets stamped: RETURN TO SENDER.

"Oberwart, no goal," a grin spread across the Yugo's entire face. And Brenner noticed that the goalie had false teeth, a complete set of dentures. Because a goalie of this caliber lives dangerously, of course.

"Newspaper write: 'Hero of Klöch,'" Brenner said.

"No hero, no."

"But newspaper! Write!"

Another broad grin for the goalie now. His dentures were perched so loosely on his gums that they slipped whenever he smiled. And you could actually see the gap between his real gums and the fake gums. *I'm not saying another word to make this goalie grin*, Brenner thought. But what are you going to do. The Yugo goalie was still so happy about the Cup victory and—without Brenner even saying a word—a grin spanned his entire face again. He said: "Oberwart, no goal, extra time, no goal, penalty shootout—"

"Hero, penalty shootout, you!"

And of course, a grin—and not a smudge of Fixodent in sight: "Three shots, I bang Oberwart!"

That's people for you. Instead of speaking correctly with foreigners, they teach them the dirtiest words.

Brenner took a few steps closer to the goalie, and although he'd been careful not to step on any bones, something cracked beneath his left foot.

"You, promotion, next round!"

"Five thousand money bonus," the goalie smiled.

"Millionaire, you! Soon!"

"Before, ten years, I millionaire. Division One, Yugoslav. Big car, but the money, all—"

"Banged, I know—"

"No banged! Build house. Beautiful house. Almost the finish. But goalie, all the time the danger. Striker, brutal pig. Shoot my head, not the ball. I break everything, my head, it breaks. Three month I sleep. All fixed, silver plate. No more Division One. I play Klöch. Klöch good. Two thousand money paycheck. Send money home, more I build house. Soon I fourteen years old."

"Forty."

"Ja, forty, no fourteen. Forty! Soon, no more I play Klöch. Then shit. But I go, still. Still!"

"Oberwart, no goal, still!"

"Still! Five thousand money bonus, I send home."

"You hero."

"No hero," Brenner heard him say, followed by that terrible squeal of the bone grinder as the Yugo finally stuffed the chicken carcass into it.

Brenner was reminded of the 3,500 spectators yesterday, and how even the ones seated the farthest back could still hear Oberwart's bones cracking. Only now it sounded reversed. So, if you were to picture yourself as the striker standing there on the grass, and suddenly you heard the bones of all 3,500 spectators breaking at once—it sounded roughly like that. Not very pleasant, I have to say.

Brenner was quick to disappear now, because first of all, the excruciating noise, and second, he wanted to finally talk with the manager. He thought to himself, *what am I doing snooping around those chicken bones when I don't even have a real contract yet.*

But when he went back upstairs, the manager still wasn't there. It took all of a second for this to get under Brenner's collar. And to be honest, I can understand why. Someone calls you, beckons you here, and when you do come, she's not here.

He went up to his room, and two minutes later his things were packed. Because that's how it is sometimes with the good-natured sort: once they get angry, there's no turning back.

It wouldn't have been Brenner, though, if something didn't get in the way. As he was standing outside in the parking lot, he thought to himself, *old man Löschenkohl, there's an upstanding old man for you, he's been punished enough, and I'll just go and quickly say goodbye to him now.*

He noticed that only one car was parked in front of the entrance to the restaurant, a silver trophy car—because before noon, nothing going on, of course. And as Brenner went walking back inside, he heard a loud cry coming from the dining room, and when he opened the door to the dining room, he saw the waitress and old man Löschenkohl and a man he didn't recognize but who definitely didn't look like a Porsche driver. Now, you're going to say, what's a Porsche driver supposed to look like, then? Anyway, not like Löschenkohl's son.

"My wife's disappeared!" he shouts, right at Brenner.

"And you are—"

"Löschenkohl," Löschenkohl's son says and offers Brenner his hand. "You don't know where my wife's at, either?"

Brenner was struck by how soft his hand was, and above all, how at first glance Löschenkohl junior looked nothing like his father. An unpleasant man, that you could tell right away. The way he talked, you know—insulting and demanding at the same time. And so fat and bloated that, next to him, his purpled father looked damn healthy.

No wonder he didn't resemble his father, though. Because his father was born in 1929, and he'd enlisted as a sixteen-year-old during the final days of the War. And compared to those who didn't come back, Löschenkohl was well-served by his mangled lower abdomen. And maybe later, that even proved to be part of the secret to his success—it's often the case with these ambitious business types that they're emboldened by a minor set back like that. Anyway, shortly after the War he married a woman who already had a son. Who he was now giving a dressing-down to: "She'll turn back up. It's not the first time she's disappeared for a few days."

"But she called me the day before yesterday. Said I absolutely had to come this morning. So that I could talk with the detective."

He had to be between forty and fifty, but somehow he reminded Brenner of the baby that Oberascher's wife had with Schmeller, and everybody knew about it—well, except for Oberascher. And now old man Löschenkohl was really giving his son a talking to, like he was a small child:

"The bigger problem is that she called Herr Brenner here. And now she herself isn't even here. And nothing's been settled, not even how much Herr Brenner charges."

The giant baby looked at Brenner now with an injured expression—and all the more aggressive for it, said, "Charge whatever you want."

"The Porsche," Brenner nearly said, just as a joke.

But he thought better of it because—a serious situation. Two streams of tears had started forming in Löschenkohl junior's alcoholic eyes. And so Brenner thought to himself: *better if I don't make a joke.* Even though he'd come to deeply regret it later.

CHAPTER 3

Back before everybody could afford a TV, people went to the bar to watch TV. That, of course, turned into a real meet-and-greet, let me tell you. World Cup in Mexico—all of Klöch was at Löschenkohl's. And not everybody even got a seat when the Brazilians dizzyingly played the Italians.

Four to one—I still know it to this day—and all of Klöch on Brazil's side because Pelé, needless to say, a wizard. And very black, he was a very dark black man, because there are lighter ones, too, but Pelé, black as coal. And white eyes that sparkled, and an artist—you just don't find that anymore today.

And you're not apt to find it anymore, either, none too quickly, because—them over there, they're doing far too well for themselves. And these days if you grow up in a slum, you've already got everything—color TV, VCR—they've got it all already, people in slums. And so a boy doesn't apply himself to his kicking that much anymore—unless it's a real slum, the motivation's simply lacking. And let's say he even goes on to become a decent soccer player—no Pelé, though.

They could only dream of color TV back then at Löschen-kohl's. And with black-and-white, well, you were just glad if you could even get a picture at first because—often just sound, no picture. And then it'd just be picture, no sound. Or a compromise, bad picture but a little bit of sound. Or, you'd have those pesky stripes, half the picture above the stripes, half the picture below—and Pelé walking on his own head in his Pumas.

But that was a long time ago, and people have had their own TVs at home for some time now. And those people who were young then are old today. With every World Cup, you think: another four years have gone by, life is but a flash. You buy a radio, then a TV, then a VCR. And then you order a fax machine and the fax mechanic rings your doorbell and you open up the door, but it's not the fax mechanic—no, it's the Bone Man come to pick you up. Isn't this the way it is, if we're being honest with ourselves?

Don't get glum, though. Because even if everything's changed, one thing today's still the same as it's always been. Every fourth Friday of the month, *Aktenzeichen XY* on TV. And that's the reason, too, why all of Klöch was back at Löschenkohl's again on this Friday night—to watch TV. Because whenever the town of Klöch gets a mention on TV, you go to Löschenkohl's. Because, these days, when everybody's got everything at home—needless to say, no fun watching TV by yourself.

A crowd like this, though—old man Löschenkohl couldn't remember the last time there'd been so many people here, not since Christmas '57, when they'd first set the TV up. Although Klöch had a hundred and twenty-three more residents back then. Because the young people don't stay in Klöch anymore, they disappear off into the city or god knows where.

But of those who do still live in Klöch, they were nearly all there. Even a lot of kids, because these days kids are allowed to watch everything on TV. So you can't be surprised when they shoot off your skull, right from the playpen.

The waitresses were under pressure, don't even ask. Four half-chickens here, a table full of pork knuckles there, six beers over there, and another slice of the house torte, and french fries for the kids. And needless to say, each more impatient than the last: Where's my pork knuckle, what's with the lemonade, what's going on with my schnitzel, do you have to slaughter the chicken first or what?

Then, the *Aktenzeichen XY* theme song, and instantly, everybody silent. No shushing, no nothing, it was absolutely quiet in the dining room. Because the skin of a chicken on its way to the fryer is nothing compared to the goosebumps you get from the sound of the *Aktenzeichen XY* theme song.

But as everyone was waiting for Eduard Zimmermann to start talking, Jacky started up instead—from the back of the room, and loud, as if the entire town of Klöch had come to listen to him: "Eduard Zimmermann always looks the same. Here's a guy who doesn't change. I'd like to think he's an old criminal who cleared out a money train once and then had his face operated on so that no one would recognize him. And now he doesn't change anymore."

Brenner knew Jacky already. The son of Löschenkohl's bathroom attendant spent the entire day leaning against the bar with a beer in his hand and talking to people. The Klöch townsfolk were starting to turn around now, out of annoyance, but Jacky wasn't finished yet.

"Wouldn't be a bad hideout if he was hiding out on *Aktenzeichen* of all places. In the lion's den. On the other hand,

though, what with fingerprinting, they'd get him right away—
and off to prison with Eduard the face-lifter."

But, now: "Shhh!" and "Quiet!" and "Shut it!" Those were
the polite ones. Brenner was surprised that they cut Jacky off
like that. Because he actually liked Jacky. His first day there
he'd even thought that Jacky was the junior manager. And to
be honest, not exactly a surprise that Brenner would come up
with an idea like that.

Jacky was good-looking, in that Italian-lover type of way
that women dream about—only later to be disappointed by
his character, but please, I could care less. Anyway, at the age
of thirty, Jacky already had silver streaks in his black hair and
always had a blazer on. That alone gave off a managerial vibe.
That and the fact that he chatted with everybody who came in
as if he owned the place, of course.

Old man Löschenkohl leaned over the bar now and whis-
pered something in Jacky's ear. Then, it was quiet. Because the
old man was known for keeping the peace. When a drunkard
became a nuisance, it was: pay up and out you go. Jacky caught
on quick, and Eduard Zimmermann could begin.

First, a roundup of the cases from the previous episode:
they caught a German money-launderer in the French-
speaking part of Switzerland. Needless to say, the French
Swiss—no pardon, but be a dear and see that you get home to
your high-security prison. Otherwise, not much came out of
the last episode, so they started right in on the new cases.

"Over to you, Sabine," Eduard Zimmermann said, because
it's a real family man who puts his own daughter on the lead
story. Sabine was hunting down criminals now, too, a clean-cut
girl, and she got to announce the first murder.

And so the first segment got underway. There are always three segments, and in between they use mugshots to look for some minor crook, but the case reenactments—always the high point. Usually one rape segment, one murder segment, and then often there's a segment where someone just barely escapes—alas only to become paralyzed.

The first segment, though, wasn't the Klöch segment. The dining room could relax a little now. Because a sixteen-year-old schoolgirl had gone missing. This you've got to picture for yourself. She rode the school bus to school every day—so her parents thought. In reality, though, high-class prostitute in Hamburg, my dear swan. And this is her purse, and please contact the police in Neumünster with any relevant information, ten-thousand-mark reward.

Normally the Klöch folk would've been excited. But today, they were only interested in their own segment. The second segment, though, still not Klöch. And then the third. Unbearable tension as Eduard Zimmermann said, "A particularly mysterious crime was uncovered in May of last year in Styra, Austria."

Um, he really shouldn't have said that. He should've done his research beforehand into how it's pronounced. "It's pronounced 'Styr-i-a,' not 'Styra,'" several tables started cursing right away. Because when you live in a small region of a small country these days, you don't just let a syllable get taken away like that.

But maybe it wasn't so much the syllables. Maybe it was more the apprehension, causing them to lash out. Eduard Zimmermann didn't let himself get needled, though: "Reporting from our Vienna studio, Peter Nidetzky."

"He's aged since the moon landing," Jacky said. Because, surely you remember how Nidetzky had been the TV commentator for the 1969 moon landing. After the moon landing fell out of fashion, though, Nidetzky was only allowed to cover dressage. And say what you will, but dressage is no moon landing. With *Aktenzeichen XY*, Nidetzky still only gets put on the minor scenes, briefly on location in Vienna, but rarely a slick case. Used to be Konrad Tönz reporting from Switzerland, maybe he'd occasionally get a slick case, but Vienna I don't much remember.

And so, needless to say, today was Peter Nidetzky's big day. Years of only dressage, now his voice was about as nervous as it'd been on the day of the first moon landing.

"Klöch is a sleepy little hamlet in East Styria, perched snug at the border of Hungary and Slovenia. In Austria, an idyll is associated with this landscape of softly rolling hills, an idyll the likes of which can scarcely be found in this day and age, even in the most pristine meadows. Not too far from this well-known Styrian Tuscany, Klöch's Wine Road has been enjoying increased popularity in recent years. It's here that you'll find numerous sights worthy of a day-trip, as well as places to stop for a bite, or to sample the new local wines at the rustic *Buschenschanken* in the area. The largest and best known of which is the Löschenkohl Grill, situated right in Klöch, a town of just one thousand souls—and it was here that a discovery was made last year, suggesting that it's anything but a perfect world down here."

The Klöchians should've gone down in the record books for this, guaranteed: five hundred people in one room, but not a sound, because no one dared gnaw on their drumsticks. They sat as though welded to their seats, not one sip of one beer, no nothing, as Peter Nidetzky spoke in his serious voice about Klöch.

And that bit about the perfect world. Practically fouling his own nest. Why you would make yourself unpopular, even in the animal kingdom—don't even ask. Because the people of Klöch were in agreement about all that with the bones having been an outside job.

But then, the reenactment got under way, and the speaker with the deep voice, you know what I'm talking about: "Monday, October twenty-third, 1995. Klöch, Province of East Styria. The Löschenkohl Grill: a widely popular destination for daytrippers."

Now, this was a peculiar experience for the Klöchites. These days, when you see something on TV, you automatically live inside it somehow. And on TV Löschenkohl's was shown from the outside. But the Klöch folk were sitting there, inside of Löschenkohl's. A strange feeling to be simultaneously inside and outside, practically a mental split.

Maybe that was the reason why Egger spilled his beer at that moment, I don't know.

Brief excitement, but then the Löschenkohl's interior was shown, and old man Löschenkohl appeared. But not the real Löschenkohl—who was standing like a Kaiser behind the bar, and constantly fiddling with the volume on the remote control so that everything could be heard at the ideal volume all the time. No, on TV, an actor, of course, so they were just pretending like it was the real Löschenkohl.

"Sixty-seven-year-old Friedrich Löschenkohl has been running a grill at this location ever since he was a young man.

Over the course of the years, he's built what started out as a modest snack bar into a full-scale gastronomic business."

The actor playing Löschenkohl was now handing a patron a fried chicken, nice and crispy—even on TV you could tell. The actor looked nothing like Löschenkohl at all, though, not one bit. He was a real gnome compared to the nearly six-foot-tall proprietor with the remote control in his hand. Although the Styrian tuxedo was spot-on, green lapels and all. The actor was far too chatty, though, so that was off. The real Löschenkohl was a pure stoic, you know, more Buddhist-oriented.

Then, there was a sudden burst of excitement in the Löschenkohl dining room.

"As in most provinces, there is a rather limited range of things to do in one's free time. As such, an even greater emphasis is placed on the local organizations—above all, soccer."

For this they had filmed the actual Klöch soccer team in practice, as the Haller boy took a shot on goal—a sweet shot, I've got to hand it to him. And the Haller boy—crowning point of his life, don't even ask. But the goalie was played by an actor again, you could tell right away, because this guy wasn't the type to merit a parade.

"Because of its proximity to the border, this minor-league club can draw upon a proud legionary contingent. The star of the team is goalkeeper Goran Milovanovic from the former Yugoslavia."

Now the goalie was portrayed walking down the steps to the basement of Löschenkohl's.

"When Goran Milovanovic isn't standing in the goal for FC Klöch, he works at the Löschenkohl Grill. Because Löschenkohl's is known throughout the region for its fried chicken, the business generates many bones. These bones are then put through a bone-grinding machine located in the cellar of the inn. Among Goran Milovanovic's tasks: manning the bone-grinder."

Now the actor-Milovanovic was shown turning on the machine.

"When, on the afternoon of October twenty-third, Goran Milovanovic went about his duties as usual, he made a gruesome discovery."

The actor playing Milovanovic reached into a mound of chicken bones and pulled out a human femur bone, including the knee, from the machine.

They pulled a good trick with that one, though. They showed the knee joint in a close-up in the Yugo's hands, as he bent it back and forth a little. And all of a sudden, they weren't the Yugo's hands holding the knee joint anymore, but Peter Nidetsky's, back in the studio, and the segment was over.

"Yes, ladies and gentlemen," Nidetsky said, "it was this very knee that Goran Milovanovic found, and further search efforts turned up an even greater number of human bones, which, as the forensic analysis has revealed, came from a middle-aged man. The bones are the only evidence we have in this highly mysterious case. We're searching not just for the perpetrator— of even greater urgency is our search for the victim. Particularly important to us are missing persons from that point in time, who, to this day, haven't been reported to the police."

"If only every one of us who went missing got reported to the police!"

That was Jacky again who said that. And he was right. As if I even have to say that Jacky was often right. He was more often right in his beer stupor than someone who's always sober. And it's the simple truth, even if you don't want to hear it: every other young person down here disappears, more or less, overnight. Out into the great wide world, as a waiter bound for Tirol, or a construction worker in Linz.

Saudi Arabia, less so. It's got its bonuses, but you have to commit to a certain number of years. Nothing's lacking down there. Women, they've got it all there—and back home you've got money in the bank. You'd like to think that after a few years you come home and you've got it made. But then, when you do come home, you find you're already more used to Saudi Arabia—often the case that you can't find your way back into normal life anymore.

I know of a case like this in the town of Straden—screwed the neighbor's kid, just a seventeen-year-old boy. They caught him, the kid went to Graz—I don't know what ever happened to him, but that was twenty years ago. They found the Straden-gone-Saudi a few days later, dead in his workshop. Needless to say, rumors. Just a way of explaining how it can be a problem when you stray too far from home.

A restlessness was gradually resuming in the dining room now. The Klöchites were disappointed about there not being anything new on *Aktenzeichen*, not one thing, but of course there hadn't been anything—nothing they hadn't known themselves for some time already.

And then Nidetsky went on about Horvath, who, if it were up to Klöch, could go to hell. "In connection with this case, the Graz Criminal Investigation Bureau is also interested in the disappearance of this man whom you see pictured here. This is renowned artist Gottfried Horvath. After attaining considerable fame, nationally and internationally, he returned to his hometown in East Styria a few years ago. Other artists have followed in his wake, buying up area farms, which, over time, had become unprofitable. Thus, the East Styria of today is home to a not insignificant artists' colony. Nearly one year ago, Gottfried Horvath disappeared without a trace. There's been no sign of him to this day."

When Nidetsky signed back over to Eduard Zimmermann, old man Löschenkohl turned off the TV. The waitresses had it even worse now than before the show. Half of Klöch wanted the check, the other half urgently needed a beer, and those who'd paid their checks were standing around in the way as they were leaving.

All over the place, it was being staunchly debated, and needless to say, Brenner pricked up his ears. Because if you want to be a detective in this day and age, you've got to listen to everything, of course, even if it's a bunch of nonsense. But the problem, of course, is when people stop spewing their own nonsense and just repeat the nonsense they hear on the news.

The Klöch folk were all more or less in agreement now that the bones had come from down there, i.e. Yugoslavia. Well, ex-. Probably a human trafficking cartel. Refugees suffocating in the trunk of the car, they have to unload them somewhere— listen, that's how it must've been.

Then, Jacky had to go and bring up the businessman from Graz. Some time ago, when the war was still going on, he turned up here at Löschenkohl's and was always having meetings with young men. Because he'd been recruiting young Austrians and Germans who were bored at home to become soldiers for the Yugos.

When Löschenkohl heard Jacky's remark, though, he interrupted: "I sent him packing so fast, he kicked up a cloud of dust. I couldn't have known at first what kind of business he was doing on my premises."

Brenner was struck by how, the more his patrons wallowed in the horror stories of a war that had taken place just a few kilometers south, the grimmer old man Löschenkohl appeared. It didn't surprise him, either, because Brenner's first day there Jacky had told him that fifty years ago the Yugoslavs had shot Löschenkohl's balls off. And it can't have brought him any joy to be reminded of it again and again because of the recent war—to make matters worse, in his own chicken joint, which, over the decades, he'd built up like a fortress against his terrible past.

"But the part about the health inspectors you didn't tell Zimmermann about!" Jacky laughed and gave old man Löschenkohl's shoulder a punch. You could tell right away that Jacky was already pretty drunk.

"They already knew about it," old man Löschenkohl said stiffly.

"Then, why didn't they say that part? Did you tell them they were only allowed to film here in the restaurant if they didn't include the bit about the health inspectors? You old dog!"

Jacky was such a typical human being, you know, the kind who starts to get belligerent when he's drunk. An otherwise nice person—not another one like him—but drunk, a nasty guy just gunning for a fight.

"It couldn't happen anymore anyway, the health inspectors finding something here. With the big bone-grinder downstairs, there's nothing there anymore."

"Yeah, it's a real pity!" Jacky acted excited. "There could still be more human bones down there, and no one would know because Milo crumbles 'em right into the machine."

"Leave Milo out of it, Jacky."

"Where's Milo even at?"

It didn't strike anyone as strange that Milovanovic wasn't there. Even though he was the one who'd mainly been featured on the TV, i.e. the evening's hero. Then again, he didn't understand much German, and anyway—as a Yugoslav, he couldn't have known how popular the show was.

By the same token, the Klöchites couldn't have known that they'd lose the next game in the Cup, seven to zero, because no trace of their mighty goalkeeper would be found.

CHAPTER 4

When you run through the ranks of a soccer team these days, it's often a difficult question, who's the most important. One person might say the coach, another person says the king of the goal. And then, you can't forget the captain, and today's latest theory: the collective is everything, and the star's just a liability.

After FC Klöch's victory in the Cup, needless to say, some outsiders believed goalkeeper Milovanovic was the most important. But not so.

Naturally, some of us down here think Schorsch the equipment manager is just a stuffed shirt. But I have to say, just because Schorsch hasn't been seen without his Motorola in three years, that doesn't make him a stuffed shirt. And Schorsch was right in saying: "As equipment manager, it's up to me to take care of this and that. I'd be in a fix without my phone."

So it didn't bother him one bit when a couple of know-it-alls made fun of him for it. Because anyone who knows his way around soccer knows that there wouldn't be an FC Klöch without him. And anyone who doesn't know his way around soccer wouldn't be interested in Schorsch anyway.

And this afternoon's practice would prove all over again just how important Schorsch truly was.

The players had just taken shots on goal, and there are a few of them who've got a powerful shot, I've got to admit. Because our village youth—maybe you're apt to turn your nose up at them, and it goes without saying, not all of them have a delicate touch, technically speaking. Shooting, though, powerful.

"And one more time!" Coach Ferdl bellowed, even though the players hadn't given any indication of exhaustion. On the contrary. Because they'd been sitting all day at the office. Still farmers in terms of genetics, lineage—but farming's dying out today, so the boys have to go into the office. Now, they've got power, hereditarily speaking, but don't know what to do with it. They're just happy if they're able to at least thrash a ball into a net come evening time.

"And one more time!"

The players had gotten used to how, apart from this sentence, their coach didn't say much. But as defenseman Dollinger shot the ball—and with it, the goalie—into the net, the coach looked a little fiercer than usual. Because he was still just a young, slender chive of a goalie. Dollinger shot at him from a distance of ten meters—needless to say, it blew him into the goal.

"And one more time!"

The coach rallied the goalie into getting up. But it cost him some authority not to grab the weakling with his own two hands and toss him right into the showers. The young goalie was the last person whose fault it was that Cup Hero Milovanovic still hadn't shown up in the three days since *Aktenzeichen* aired.

When the players shot two of the three training balls over the fence and into the river, though, the coach had finally had enough. He worked himself into such a fit of rage that half the players had thoughts of finding another club to play for going through their heads.

And that was the moment when everyone could see all over again who the most important player on FC Klöch truly was. Because that was the moment when Equipment Manager Schorsch came running out onto the field. He was holding his cell phone in his left hand, but in his right hand he was carrying something far more important.

"It's not so bad, those two balls that went wide," he yelled into the first seconds of silence following the thunderstorm.

And, as a matter of fact, in the bulging burlap sack that was thrown over his right shoulder, there were exactly thirty balls, because these days even the sacks are nearly bigger than the equipment managers.

Now, you can't forget what it means to a soccer player, the sight of a sack like this that's bulging full of soccer balls. Because, as a soccer player, you have a relationship to the ball. It used to be the brown leather balls, and then the black-and-white leather balls, and then the colorful leather balls, and then the completely white balls covered in synthetic leather. The balls may have changed, but there's one thing that never will.

If a crisis breaks out during practice, then Equipment Manager Schorsch comes running onto the field with his burlap sack of balls. Because he knows that when the players see the sack, well, the moment he sends those balls thundering onto the field they're really going to feel it. You've got to imagine a pounding waterfall of leather balls. And at that moment when the players feel the waterfall—crisis averted.

So, Equipment Manager Schorsch was surprised, of course, when he went running toward the players with that enormous sack of balls, and yet the players' expressions only got more sullen.

"It's really not that bad, two balls in the river," the equipment manager yelled out again in encouragement, and he turned his back a little to the players so that they could see the sack full of balls better.

The better the players saw the sack, though, the paler they turned. And not one of them said a word. Even the coach was quiet now, but the equipment manager just took that as a measure of success. That the coach didn't lay into the players a second time, as is often the case in a thunderstorm. Nonetheless, Schorsch's trick wasn't quite working this time on the players—no way he could've failed to notice that now.

"What's up today?" he yells and swings the sack over his shoulder like Old St. Nick.

"The bag," Udo Sommerer says. He'd just moved up last season from the youth league to competition play, and why Udo of all people was the first to find his tongue again, I don't know, either.

"What about the bag?" Schorsch says, and sticks his cell phone into the elastic waistband of his sweat pants because he needs his other hand to untie the bag.

"The bag!" two, three others are shouting now because the equipment manager still doesn't see it.

"What about the bag?" the equipment manager shouts back. He couldn't see it, because the man doesn't have eyes on his back.

But then, all of the sudden, he felt something moist against his bare calf. Because, in the cold of the locker room overnight, the thirty-first ball had only made an undetectable stain. As the equipment manager dragged it through the afternoon heat, though, it began to bleed a little. And by the time the equipment manager got to the penalty box where the players were, the shape of a head was already showing through the burlap a little. Now, I wouldn't necessarily compare Schorsch's burlap sack with a shroud like they found down in Turin. But a little like that, just so you can picture it, how the nose and the eye sockets were imprinting themselves more and more clearly. And as the thirty-first ball started dripping down the bare calf of the equipment manager, he finally noticed it, too.

And so, once again, you see how important it is for an equipment manager to always have a cell phone. Because fifteen minutes later, the Radkersburger Gendarmerie were already on the soccer field. And it didn't even take an hour for the Graz police to get there, either.

But the Graz police could've taken their sweet time because the Radkersburger Gendarmerie—highly competent. They didn't leave any work left undone. The victim was clearly identified, because everybody—except for the young goalie— recognized the head. It belonged to FC Feldbach striker Ortovic, and just a few months earlier they'd lost to Feldbach, one to zero. Ironic twist of fate: it'd been a header by Ortovic of all things—off a corner kick in the seventy-sixth minute, and at the far corner of the goal, Ortovic had shot right up like a rocket. And now, a thing like this.

By the time the Graz police showed up, the Radkersburger Gendarmerie had already searched the entire grounds, too. But no trace of Ortovic's body. They didn't even have to break into the locker room because the window there's always open so that it doesn't get too dank. And that's usually not a problem in Klöch. Nothing goes walking off on its own here. And walking off wasn't the problem anyway. No, the problem was that something new had shown up.

Not a single trace, either, the Klöch Gendarmerie reported to the Graz police. Then they searched a little more for fingerprints and footprints, but nothing much came of it.

By five-thirty the whole nightmare was already over. The Radkersburger Gendarmerie returned to their posts down at the speed-trap by the north off-ramp. The police pathologist took Ortovic's head with him for further examination. And Dreher, the criminologist's assistant, was more than happy to be sent home by his boss, Kaspar Krennek. Because it was his last day of work before a four-week vacation, and he'd already been sweating blood all afternoon that he might have to postpone his trip to Thailand on account of some damned soccer player's head.

Kaspar Krennek was an unusual boss in this regard, though. He enjoyed playing the deputy to his subordinates. Because all that office and politics and eating asparagus all the time—in the long run, that's a small death sentence, too.

When Kaspar Krennek turned up at Löschenkohl's, needless to say, people recognized him right away. And not just because half the soccer team had gotten there before him and had already given everybody the blow-by-blow about the incident in question. No, Kaspar Krennek was known throughout the country. Because ever since he'd joined the Graz police force—and it's going on nearly ten years now—he's been coddled by the newspapers.

You should know, his father was August Krennek, the famous post-War Hamlet. Now, the son becoming a cop, that was a certain kind of rebellion against the father. But when he made a career of it as a detective, well, father and son finally reconciled on the father's deathbed.

And, these days, when your father's an actor, then you've got a bit of the theater bug in you, too. Even though, with Kaspar Krennek, you have to look pretty closely to discover the actor within. Because you don't notice his vanity right away. First glance: a quiet, modest man. And only on the second glance: *I am the Prince of the Murder Department.*

When, at a quarter after six, he came walking into the dining room at Löschenkohl's in his twenty-thousand-schilling leather jacket, he didn't act coy for long.

"Where's the junior manager?" he asked the first server he saw.

"What junior manager?"

Because Gudrun had only been working at Löschenkohl's for a few weeks, and she'd only caught sight of the junior manager maybe once. Just then, though, the head waitress came to her aid.

"Is it Paul you're looking for?"

"It's Paul whom I'd like to speak with."

Kaspar Krennek had learned from his father that a man must express himself with precision. And that "speaking with" hasn't meant "looking" for some time now.

"To speak," the head waitress said in a tone as if to say: *don't get clever with me, you Schlaumeier.* "Paul doesn't live here."

"Where does he live, then?"

"You'll have to ask his father that."

"So, he can be spoken with."

"Not until I find him," the waitress smirked and disappeared into the kitchen.

Krennek was a little surprised by the cheery mood of the place. On the other hand, there's just a certain cheerfulness about people after a glimpse at death has sent them filling their pants.

Two minutes later the waitress returned. But not with old man Löschenkohl. With a man roughly Kaspar Krennek's age. But a head shorter and a foot and a half wider. And with skin like sandpaper.

"Brenner."

Krennek was a little annoyed at first that the headstrong waitress had been able to lure him out of his reserve so quickly. Now he was glad to have won back his modesty again. He put out his hand to Brenner, and out of sheer reservation, didn't quite get to introducing himself before Brenner said, "You're looking for Herr Löschenkohl."

This time, though, Krennek didn't correct him—even if his father was rolling over in his grave.

"Unfortunately, Herr Löschenkohl isn't here today," Brenner said.

"Which one, junior or senior?"

"Neither one's here. Junior's never here anyway. And the old man drove to Graz today for a doctor's appointment. He'll be back first thing tomorrow."

Doctor's appointment. Brenner couldn't have known what a scare he gave Krennek with that one. Because ever since Krennek was a kid, he'd had the *idée fixe*, if you will, that on his fortieth birthday, he would die of cancer. And he was already pushing thirty-nine now. Needless to say, he didn't dare go to the doctor for a checkup.

The two of them took a seat at a table, and after two beers they didn't even notice anymore that everyone in the dining room was staring at them. And about that I've really got to say: rarely have a police inspector and a private detective worked so well together.

Brenner told the inspector about the Löschenkohl manager who'd disappeared, and Krennek told Brenner why it was so urgent for him to speak with the old man. Because of the bribery scandal that shook up the province's minor leagues six months earlier. In which Löschenkohl junior bribed a Feldbach striker. Namely, Ortovic, whose head someone had cut off and put in FC Klöch's ball sack.

At ten, the inspector set about making his way home. "If you see old man Löschenkohl, tell him I'll be paying him a visit in the morning."

"Tomorrow you'll meet him for sure," Brenner said in farewell.

Brenner didn't move from the table while the waitress locked up the restaurant behind Kaspar Krennek. She had a coarse face—not from age, because she wasn't that old yet. Just not a delicate face, a coarse one. But a fine human being. A thickset body, though, just like professional soccer players at the end of their careers. They're training less, but eating the same amount—naturally, they let themselves go a little. Needless to say, that red leather skirt of hers was a risky affair now.

But that only proves yet again that you can't judge a person by appearances alone. The only thing that Brenner didn't understand was: where did this woman find her lovers night after night? Because what he overheard coming from her room—I don't wish to describe it, but G-rated it was not.

"Where's the boss been this whole time?" Brenner asked her.

"Not back yet from his checkup."

"I'm not talking about the old man. The manager's husband."

"Not Porsche Pauli, though."

Porsche Pauli. That got Brenner thinking to himself, *I'm glad I don't live out here in the country, because at least I don't have a nickname like that.*

"The way I see it, everybody's my boss. So I'm not the type to call the shots here. When you're a waitress, everybody's your boss anyway. Porsche Pauli, though, is not my boss."

"You mean, the old man's still the boss?"

"The manager's the boss. But now I need to hurry up and eat my frankfurters, before they get cold," the waitress says and walks back over to the bar.

"But the manager is, in fact, just the daughter-in-law," Brenner said, while she prepared her frankfurters at the bar.

"And the only one here who can run a business," the waitress said. "Or did you think that Porsche Pauli could run a business like this?"

"Why don't you and your frankfurters have a seat over here with me?"

"If it wouldn't bother you," the waitress said and walked back to the table with her steaming plate of sausages. And she nearly had to spit the first bite out—that's how hot they were. But one, two hasty chewing motions with an open mouth and a few controlled breaths and down it went.

"There's nothing better than frankfurters. When they're hot, that is."

"Those are hot, all right," Brenner said and stared in amazement as she gobbled down the next bite and the next, each far too hot.

"They have to be."

"Maybe that's why I've never liked the taste of frankfurters. Because I always eat them too cold."

"In Frankfurt they call them 'wieners,' and in Vienna, they're 'frankfurters,'" the waitress said through a mouthful. "And do you know why?"

"Nobody wants to be the sausage."

"That would explain it, too," the waitress laughed. "But I'm going to tell it to you like this: a Viennese butcher invented the sausage. And his name was Frankfurter."

"You'd like to think they've just always existed."

"No, no. Invented. In Vienna. By Frankfurter."

"Do you always eat your sausages without a bun?"

"Always! Never eat a sausage on a bun."

"If you like sausages so much, then Porsche Pauli must be your best friend."

"You can say that again, dumplin'—that Porsche Pauli's a real weenie. And a cold one at that," the waitress laughed, because, for her, it was evidently time to drop the formalities.

But Brenner was still a little uncertain about whether he was ready to do the same. Maybe you're familiar with this, when someone gets chummy all of a sudden, but you can't quite bring yourself to reciprocate. So Brenner simply changed the subject: "Where's Porsche Pauli been this whole time?"

The waitress gave an ambivalent shrug of her shoulders.

"Since the bribery scandal broke, he doesn't dare show his face back home anymore."

"You think he had something to do with Ortovic's death… dumplin'?"

Ah, that first attempt at familiarity. It always tickles the palate a bit, not unlike when you put something too hot in your mouth.

"Don't make me laugh," was all the waitress said.

And then they heard someone unlocking the door from the outside. Because there was one small detail that Brenner hadn't been entirely honest with the inspector about.

"Train had a fifteen-minute delay," old man Löschenkohl said, cursing as he came in.

The old man sat down at Brenner's table, and the waitress brought him a glass of water.

"Will you join me in having a bite to eat?" he asked Brenner.

Needless to say, a double opportunity for Brenner now. First of all, he wanted to see if he could get Löschenkohl talking a little before he told him the story about Ortovic's head. That way, maybe he'd find something else out about the bribery scandal surrounding the old man's son. Second of all: "A couple of frankfurters."

Because even though he wasn't the least bit hungry, the waitress's appetite was contagious.

"Hey, Toni, a couple frankfurters, no bun, one beer!" Löschenkohl yelled to the waitress from across the deserted restaurant.

"And for you?" Brenner asked.

"I'm not eating anything else today. The doctor said I have to watch my eating. It's all getting to be too much for me. I can only hope that you'll find my daughter-in-law soon. The business is just too much for me to handle on my own."

"And your son?"

How long do frankfurters take? If you want them to be good, at least ten minutes. Because you don't actually cook them, or else they'll split open on you. Just until they're heated through. And that's where a lot of people go wrong, they don't let them simmer long enough. And if they're supposed to be really hot, then you've got to let them simmer for at least ten minutes.

Now why's that so important? Because the whole time the frankfurters were cooking, old man Löschenkohl didn't say a word. Although he understood the question perfectly well. No answer for at least ten minutes. And when the frankfurters arrived, they were steaming—you could tell right away that, back in the kitchen, the waitress had personally seen to it that they be simmered long enough.

Brenner bit fearlessly into the sausage, though, just so he could say to old man Löschenkohl: "Now I've gone and burned my mouth."

"You should wait a little longer."

Brenner nodded and blew on his steaming frankfurter, but before he took a bite he said, "And how much longer should I wait before you answer my question about your son?"

"About my son? So you didn't burn your mouth after all. No, it's just that—I'm just, you know. In my head."

"Don't get me wrong. It's just that if I'm going to find your daughter-in-law, then I need to know as much as possible about her. And her husband, too, of course."

"All right, okay."

"I was down on the soccer field today. Practice."

"Mm-hmm, soccer, the boys, practice."

"I got to talking a little with the coach there," Brenner lied. "He told me your son's mixed up in a bribery scandal."

"A bunch of nonsense."

"Is it not true?"

Now, picture Brenner feeling with his tongue for whether little patches of skin were peeling off the roof of his mouth— that's how hot the frankfurters were.

"Unfortunately, yes, it's true that my son got into that mess."

"And he hasn't been home since?"

"No, no. It's been longer than that since he's been here. Got married four years ago. So he hasn't been here since then."

"But his wife still runs the business here?"

"Yeah. His wife stayed. But him, always on the move. Married a competent woman. Because she's a good one who's always had to work. And him, a disappearing act."

"What was your son doing that whole time, then?"

"You'll have to ask him that. Nothing good. Only comes home when he needs money. Or now. He's worried about his wife, of course. Doesn't care all year long, but when she disappears, that's too much for him. For once he'll have to do some work himself. Instead of tooling around in his Porsche."

Then Löschenkohl got very quiet again. Brenner was starting to notice just how often the old man could drop off from one second to the next.

A poor old man, Brenner thought, *must be awfully lonely, and why should I keep pestering him about his son. When he won't tell me the truth anyway.* A father telling you the truth about his son—you're not apt to experience that very often. Because assuming he'd even be able to—where are you going to find a father today who even knows something about his son? You see, right back where we started.

When Brenner had finished his sausages, he simply got up and left the silent old man sitting there. But it was at that exact moment—or maybe was it because the soft jolt of the table woke him back up?—that old man Löschenkohl said: "Ferdl."

"What Ferdl?"

"From the soccer team, the coach. You did say that he's the one who told you all that."

"The coach, right. His name's Ferdl?"

"He's a bus driver by day. They're always taking bus trips down Yugo-ways. Senior citizens, *gratis*. So, they don't have to pay anything for the trip, the seniors."

"And then they sell them some kind of miracle pillow for twenty thousand schillings," Brenner said, because his Aunt Emmi back in Puntigam went on one of these trips and came back with a miracle pillow. Emmi wasn't sorry about the money for long, though, because she dropped dead shortly thereafter, standing in line at the Easter confessional. Sixty-seven years old, that's no age for a woman.

"Ferdl's always a real entertainer on those bus trips," Löschenkohl wasn't going to let Brenner distract him from what he wanted to say. "That man can tell jokes, unbelievable. The old widows all fall in love with him."

"It's good for business."

"But in the locker room," Löschenkohl said, a little softer now, because he's the kind of person who, just by getting a little quieter, could bring you up short. "In the locker room—and everybody down here knows it—there, it's like he's a different man. You can't get a word out of him."

"Aha."

"Do you want me to be honest with you?"

And Brenner: "If you want me to find your daughter-in-law."

And old man Löschenkohl: "Then you're going to have to be honest with me, too. Because all that about Ortovic's head was already on the seven o'clock news. You didn't need to dish up some story about Ferdl to me. Because maybe my son bribed Ortovic. But decapitate him—he doesn't have what it takes."

Brenner was just standing there, caught awkwardly between the table and the bench, because Löschenkohl had started talking to him when he was in the middle of getting up. And now, needless to say, doubly awkward. And for a full minute he didn't know: *should I sit back down or should I go, what'll look stupider?*

But old man Löschenkohl was god-knows-where in his thoughts again, and by now, Brenner realized that his left leg had fallen asleep, and so Coach Ferdl was of help to him after all:

"And one more time!" Brenner shouted silently at himself and gave his sleeping leg a jolt. Then, like a fouled kicker, he limped off to the staff's quarters.

CHAPTER 5

MAGNIFICENT DAYCATION TO SLOVENIA. ONLY 148 SCHIL-LINGS! WITH SLOVENIAN EASY LISTENING AND FOLKLORE PERFORMANCE. ROUNDTRIP TRAVEL IN STATE-OF-THE-ART CHARTER BUS WITH PANORAMIC WINDOWS.

** LADIES WILL RECEIVE: 1 LARGE HANDBAG WITH IN-TERIOR POCKET AND MATCHING COSMETICS CASE IN THIS SEASON'S LATEST FAUX-CROCODILE LOOK

** GENTLEMEN WILL RECEIVE: 1 KEYRING, 1 BILLFOLD, AND DUAL-COMPARTMENT BRIEFCASE IN THIS SEASON'S LATEST FAUX-CROCODILE LOOK

** HOME DECOR SHOW COURTESY OF THE VOGL-VERSAND FIRM, MUNICH (PARTICIPATION OPTIONAL)

WE'LL BE HANDING OUT THESE GIFTS—AND MORE!—DIRECTLY TO OUR LOYAL CUSTOMERS DURING OUR ANNI-VERSARY TRIP!

PLEASE MARK YOUR PREFERRED POINT OF DEPAR-TURE:

GLEISDORF

SINABELKIRCHEN

ILZ

RIEGERSBURG

FELDBACH (TRAIN STATION)

BAD GLEICHENBERG

HALBENRAIN

BAD RADKERSBURG (CENTRAL SQUARE)

When Brenner got on at Halbenrain, the bus was nearly full already. The driver looked a little confused, and so immediately Brenner felt like he'd been caught doing something. Because these days when you get on a crowded bus as a newcomer, you already have the feeling that the other people have just always been there. And if one of them looks at you oddly, well, it can seem like you've been caught doing something, if that's your tendency.

And Brenner had good reason to feel this way. He was afraid Coach Ferdl might recognize him and guess that Brenner wanted to get him talking.

But no chance of Ferdl recognizing anyone. And when Brenner scanned the other people on the bus, he knew right away, of course, why the confused look. Because, except for Brenner, all the passengers—practically old folks' home.

There was only one young woman there, in a bright-green suit and with dyed blond hair, but the sheer blondness of it made it look more like a straw wig.

"You must be Herr Brenner?" she said, because she was part of the bus, and Brenner didn't even have time to nod before she bellowed into a microphone: "Join me in welcoming Herr Brenner from Klöch."

Needless to say, very embarrassing, the old folks all applauding obediently. Brenner would've liked to turn right around and get off the bus, but not a chance.

"There are still three seats in the back," the hostess bellowed into her damn microphone, even though Brenner was standing all of a foot and a half away from her. Needless to say, a problem. *What am I doing in the back of the bus*, Brenner thought, *when I'd like to be having a chat with the driver*. So, real sly now, he says to the hostess:

"I don't do so well on tour buses. Couldn't I, maybe, here up front—"

You can stop right there. The seniors in the front seats, well—their pacemakers nearly leapt out of their chests when they heard that. Because they always feel terrible on buses, as a matter of fact, and now some young upstart comes along and wants to take their hard-fought seats up front away from them.

The hostess didn't even condescend to answer and Brenner went bravely to the back without any further fuss. Because Brenner knew from his time on the force that there's nothing more dangerous than old folks with canes. Cane or bayonet, once you have it stuck in your stomach, it's often just a matter of interpretation. So he consoled himself: *I'll still be able to draw Ferdl out when we stop in Maribor.*

They were barely over the border when the hostess began to spout off into her microphone. Because she had to warm up the crowd. And more importantly, pass out the gifts.

Brenner looked out the window at their surroundings, and needless to say: it looked exactly the same on this side of the border as it did on the other side of the border. Then, he noticed that on the seat-back in front of him another microphone had been mounted, and he could interrupt the hostess with it: "Thou shalt not work so hard for tips!"

His deep, godlike voice gave the seniors such a scare that several of them dropped dead on the spot. And the others weren't any better off, either, because they got eaten alive by the crocodile-skin bags that the hostess had given them.

When Brenner woke up, they were already in Maribor's Central Square.

They were given an hour's time for sightseeing in the city, and then, at one o'clock, lunch followed by shopping. Optional, of course, but the lunch was a good value, so everybody went along, well-behaved, except for one woman—and, well, she'd gotten herself lost in Maribor.

Meanwhile, the hostess and the coach had built a small stage in the dining room, and needless to say, microphones weren't in short supply. Over lunch, the seniors were getting curious about what kind of secrets awaited them.

And once the coffee was on the table, the hostess and coach set about peddling their wares—a miracle blanket that you cover yourself with and two weeks later, no more rheumatism. It cost six thousand schillings, so the five schillings that they'd already forked out for lunch—already recouped. Because the seniors who bought them, well, they all must've had terrible cases of rheumatism.

Or maybe it was just Ferdl's charm. Because the hostess took over the more informative part, but Ferdl—his commentary made the old ladies blush.

"And one more time!" Ferdl called out after every six-thousand-schilling blanket—and the next grandma would already have her new faux-crocodile bag open and would be shelling out six thousand schillings. Because you don't want to sit there looking stingy, either, like you were only taking advantage of the cheap trip, and the driver—real nice guy. Just two hours earlier they were ready to nail Brenner to the stake, but now the old folks were quick to show their magnanimous sides again.

"That last shirt didn't have any pockets," the old man sitting vis-à-vis Brenner said.

Brenner didn't quite know what he should say to that, because what do you say to an old man who makes an announcement like that. Doesn't matter anyway—the old man wasn't expecting an answer. He was the one who talked himself into buying that last shirt, and he was already making his way over to Ferdl now.

And at that moment the woman who'd gotten lost in Maribor burst into the dining room and right up onto the stage. You couldn't have looked fast enough—already had her rheumatism blanket.

"And one more time!" Ferdl called out.

Once all the blankets—and then an entire stack of gewgaws—were gone, the seniors were permitted another half an hour of walking around, and then it was back on the bus—and don't be late.

That's just Ferdl's charm—*like old man Löschenkohl was talking about*, Brenner thought. *And if I'm not quick now, then I'll be sitting in the back of the bus again, while Ferdl silently spins his steering wheel up front, and I still won't know why Löschenkohl junior bribed Ortovic.*

That's why Brenner simply stayed in his seat there in the dining room. The seniors were out strolling, and Ferdl and the hostess were up front, taking down their altar.

At first the hostess masked a dirty look. And then Ferdl did the same, but just for a few seconds. And then a blatantly dirty look from Ferdl, but just a few seconds again. And then Ferdl: "Journalist, right?"

"Why a journalist?"

"I can smell a journalist ten kilometers upwind."

"And here I didn't even feel a breeze."

Needless to say, the look. They can't kill, though—that's been proven. That's why Brenner was still alive.

Ferdl had had just about enough of these tabloid journalists. There was nothing the club needed less right now than that old bribery scandal with Ortovic getting dragged back up again.

And I've really got to congratulate Brenner on that. Because he was about to win Ferdl over with a single word.

"Oberwart," Brenner said. "Was that just the crowning point of your life, or what?"

And you should've seen it, what a difference it made to Ferdl, the topic of their victory in the Cup. You've got to picture it like this, like when the sun comes out on a cloudy day—yes, that is the best comparison. How Ferdl's expression, all of a sudden—it just really brightened up.

Because the "Portrait of the Week" series in the sports section—it had always been his boyhood dream to make it into there. And people could talk all they wanted about the senior citizens' tours, fraud or no fraud. Ferdl put all of that money into the club anyway. He would've given a thousand Miracle Blankets just to make it into the "Portrait of the Week." And now the "Portrait of the Week" was standing right in front of him in the flesh, and he'd almost been unfriendly.

"You'll have to excuse me. Nothing personal. It's just that—it's chaotic with the club right now."

Brenner just nodded.

"But you know what," Ferdl said, "let's chat about the Cup victory on the bus. Because I still have to pack up all this stuff right now."

"That'll be tough."

"Yeah, not easy. All this stuff in half an hour. We have to be back at six, though. The old folks' homes are very strict."

"For us to have a conversation on the bus, I mean, it'll be tough."

"Why's that?"

"Because you're the driver."

"Yeah, of course, I'm the driver."

"So, it'll be tough for you during the ride to come to the back of the bus, where my seat is."

All of a sudden, Ferdl got serious—the last time he'd been this serious, he was taking Ortovic's head out of the ball sack. Brenner was afraid he suspected trickery. And these days when you're a detective and you want to get something out of somebody, that's rule number one: you can't ever give him the feeling that you're tricking him. You have to trick him, of course, but you just can't give him the feeling that you're doing it. That's the art of it.

No chance of Ferdl feeling tricked, though. Because he was saying, dead-serious now: "Then, we'll find a solution."

And then, a marvelous solution. The hostess would give up her co-driver's seat to Brenner. She'd be standing practically the entire trip anyway and making empty chitchat with the people. Because she had to get them fired up for the next trip. Jealous, nevertheless, of course, Brenner getting to sit up front like that.

Brenner had a magnificent view of the countryside from right behind the panoramic windshield, and it's been said that a magnificent view is liberating for the soul. And maybe there's something to that, why it was all just tripping off his tongue now.

He was talking so snappily with Ferdl that surely you would have taken him for a sports journalist, too. And this in spite of Brenner not knowing the first thing about soccer.

"Your man in the goal, he's a real miracle worker."

"You can say that again."

"Did you discover him?"

"Milo had quit playing altogether."

Brenner didn't ask any follow-up questions. Because it had been his experience that you learn a lot more from people when you don't follow up. As soon as you do, they get wary. But if you wait patiently and aren't too interested, they'll tell you everything. But you've got to wait with feeling, and attention, sure, interest, too, even a key word here or there, but don't ever pose a question. There's a golden rule for you to take note of.

But it was Ferdl now, of all people, who didn't continue, so Brenner had no choice but to ask: "And how did he end up coming to Klöch then?"

"Milo played Division One back in Yugoslavia. So I'd always seen him on TV. Because we get the Yugo-channels down here. Can't understand a word of it, but the soccer's superb. And I was often struck by Milovanovic—he was a top goalkeeper. World class. Of course, never in his dreams did he think he might play for us. But then, five, six years ago, a Belgrade Partisans' striker smashed his skull. Usually a striker hangs back. But this one charged full-on. Jaw broken, nose broken, cheekbones broken, and, and, and—don't even ask. Intensive care and, and, and. How do you think he looked after that?"

"In a coma, too?"

"Yeah, of course, coma, and, and, and. Until they put him back together again."

"Silver plate, too?"

"Silver plate, the works. You can build a whole business off a player like Milo."

"How much did you buy Milo for?"

"Ah, okay, I see where you're going. That's good. All right, listen up. After the accident, nobody heard a word out of Milo."

"Left the building."

"Yeah, but really left. The building. Didn't hear a thing for years. I completely forgot about him. Because that's how it goes in soccer. If you're famous today, everybody celebrates you. But once you're gone, you're really gone."

"But you didn't forget about him, did you?"

"When our goalkeeper got sold off to another team last year—Kaup, he's a third-string goalie now for the Graz Sturm—that's when Milovanovic crossed my mind again. I thought to myself, *he might be healthy by now. Or at least healthy enough for Klöch.* And because I drive down there every weekend, needless to say, I've got my connections. It wasn't long before I'd found him, Milo."

"And where was he?"

"Where else would he have been? At the construction site, of course. He'd started building a house back when he was earning good money playing professional ball. Now, he's left to finish it himself."

"And it was easy to convince him?"

"Not easy, exactly. But needless to say—" the chauffeur rubbed his thumb and index finger together with relish. "He couldn't say no."

If you could've seen Ferdl like this, you would've thought they were shelling out a hundred thousand a month to Milo.

"You couldn't be paying him that much to play for Klöch,"

Brenner said, even though Milo himself had told him for a fact: two thousand schillings a month, base salary.

"Oh, he gets paid well. For a Yugo. Foreign currency exchange—he can put it all into his house."

"But he's still got to work at Löschenkohl's on the side."

"Yeah, exactly. He earns even more foreign money over at Löschenkohl's."

"So it seems. He earns a little something from the club. And then he earns a little more at Löschenkohl's. And at Löschenkohl's he's not paid too badly, either."

Löschenkohl. Löschenkohl. Löschenkohl. One thing you've got to hand to Brenner. He might be a little longer-winded than the next guy, but he'd just brought Ferdl, nice and slowly, right to where he wanted him. And now he says, "Löschenkohl junior's got his toe in the team, too."

"Had."

Pause.

"Had!" the driver says again. "Because he doesn't have a say in the team anymore."

"On account of him bribing Ortovic?"

Ferdl didn't say anything for a while now. He was only being silent, though, because that's what you do with a sad topic. And then he said, "Löschenkohl junior caused a lot of damage to our team. Nevertheless, I'm not angry at him. Because he hurt me."

"How did he hurt you?"

"Don't you know him?"

"I've only seen him."

"He's a poor bastard. Our club's president bribing Feldbach's striker. You could only dream up something like that.

It'd never happened before in the minor leagues. Not in our whole history."

"And the striker went straight to the newspapers?"

"He was an honest Yugo."

"And Löschenkohl?"

"Kicked straight out of the club. Made a nice, high arc, too. What else were we supposed to do?"

"But he didn't admit it."

"Nobody ever does. But it was obvious. I knew Ortovic personally. And I have to say, a pity, such a nice guy. And a good striker. And a favorite with the ladies, of course, because Orto, he was a real character—not very big, but a little devil, and strong as a steer."

Ferdl had a look of outright pleasure on his face as he described Ortovic. But don't get any ideas—because it's true: you often hear that about coaches, all that about the smaller boys, it's not purely athletic interest that motivates them. But a certain something else, too.

But Ferdl—never. On that I'd lay my hand in the fire. Because he was a real lady-killer himself, and frankly, when he was describing Ortovic, he saw himself in it a little, too. And if you look at it that way, it was truly from an honest heart that he said, for a second time: "A real pity about that guy."

"And so it was because of Ortovic's testimony that you threw Löschenkohl junior out of the club?"

"We had to distance ourselves from the management, of course. So that everyone would see: it was only the tip of, of, of—"

"Of the iceberg?"

"No, of—of the club, I mean. Of the management. Only the president. Just Löschenkohl."

They were driving up to the border now. No drawn-out formalities, though, because Ferdl knew the customs officer. I don't want this to come out the wrong way but—certain agreements were in place. Anyway, they waved the bus right through, and then, once they were across, the driver said, "They're always lined up here at night. Yugo-whores. Just like the soccer players who play for us, the whores earn a little foreign money, too."

All this about the foreign currency really seemed to bother Ferdl. As a chauffeur, you probably have a certain relationship to it. Really not a bad profession, and one where you can get to know a lot over time. It goes without saying, Ferdl had a good general knowledge: "The Yugo-whores are cheaper and better than the ones at home."

"Just like the soccer players," Brenner said.

"Yeah, exactly. Like the soccer players," Ferdl laughed. And then he nodded his head toward the side of the road and said, "First one's already standing there. Especially on the weekends, though, it's just teeming with them. Ortovic's girlfriend always used to stand there, too. Before she disappeared."

"Did she run out on Ortovic?"

But, now—and you see, that's what I've been trying to say this whole time! Follow-up question at the wrong moment, and just like that—it's all over.

Because it was now that Ferdl realized: Brenner wasn't a sports reporter. If he didn't even know that Yugo-striker Ortovic and his girlfriend had disappeared a few days after the bribery scandal broke. From one day to the next, as if swallowed up by the earth.

Ferdl lapsed into an icy silence from behind his steering wheel. Brenner could follow up or not follow up, and the only answer he'd get: icy Ferdl-silence. Until Brenner tickled him with the miracle blanket. That got the chauffeur finding a few choice words again.

In the end, though, he didn't know anything else, except that Ortovic, the Feldbach striker, had popped back up again two days ago. In FC Klöch's ball bag. Roughly three days after Klöch's goalkeeper Milovanovic disappeared without a trace.

CHAPTER 6

Now, this is where the story gets a little uncomfortable, of course. Because Brenner's thinking, *Ortovic's girlfriend, the missing prostitute, maybe I'll go to Radkersburg, say, to the Border-line, maybe there I'll find something out.*

Now, you're going to say, that's a good excuse. And I can just hear folks talking already: Brenner certainly didn't go un-willingly to the Borderline. And you can't hold it against any-body for thinking that. Just between us, Brenner himself wasn't entirely certain, either, *am I going for the research, per se, or is there a little, you know, too.* So I don't see why I even need to bother. Practically speaking, Brenner's only a man.

And street prostitution—needless to say, another thing altogether, and there you'd be right in saying, what was Brenner looking for at the Borderline. But when everybody's always thinking they know better, then it's up to me to be the one who says: it was here, at the Borderline of all places, that Brenner got somewhere, one decisive millimeter farther. And without this millimeter, the Bone Man might never have been caught— might still be running around Styria on a brutal rampage— and to this day mothers might not dare let their kids play in the streets. No children's bones were ever found among the bones at Löschenkohl's, of course. These days, though, if you're a mother, well, needless to say—caution, mother of all wisdom.

And it's only a handful of mothers today who realize that
it's Brenner they should be thanking for the fact that they can
let their children back out into the open countryside. And bad-
minton, and swimming, and bike riding, yes, my dears, what
fun—and all just because Brenner went to a brothel. The way
I see it: so be it if a certain something else played a part in
Brenner's decision, i.e., not one hundred percent research. Is it
so terrible, if we have a few less deaths in Styria today?

You'll have to excuse me, but it really gets on my nerves
sometimes, how sanctimonious people can be. Now, where'd
I leave off.

It was a Sunday night, two days after the bus trip to Maribor. *Because Saturday night at a brothel is just too much of a pro-
duction*, Brenner thought. *Better to go on a Sunday night, when
there aren't that many customers and it'll be easier to strike up a
conversation with the girls.*

Twenty years ago, when Brenner was still in the police
academy, he went to the cathouse a few times, because that's
what you do—young man, part of a group, you go to a cathouse once. But you can't always use a group as an excuse, because, as far as that goes, Brenner hadn't exactly been the voice
of dissent—I don't want to sugarcoat anything. But since the
academy, he hadn't had anything to do with prostitutes—well,
once, at most, in an official capacity, but not privately.

It'd been such a long time that he was a little nervous
now, buyer's anxiety, so to speak. A moment later, though, he
was already feeling right at home again, because he met an old
acquaintance at the door. Turns out, Jacky wasn't unemployed
after all—he only had time to hang around Löschenkohl's all
day long because by night he worked as a bouncer.

"Ah, so this is your business, Jacky."

"No, it's my idealism," Jacky grumbled. He was still a little sensitive, because it was only recently that he'd had to start working back at the Borderline again.

Just a month earlier he'd been thrown out by the chief physician in Graz when, out of nowhere, two of her nurses got pregnant. Supposedly, that's even why she wasn't promoted to medical director, because the people down here are always a little weird about a fifty-year-old taking a thirty-year-old lover. I don't know if there's any truth to the rumor, but it might have a speck of a kernel of a truth.

Jacky held the door open for Brenner, and then the heavy red curtains, then a black door with a round glass window, and then, of course, big surprise.

And you could see how times have changed. People always say that, especially about kids, you're supposed to see how the times change. Well, Brenner was seeing it now at the brothel. Because it was a distant echo of the brothels of twenty years ago when he'd been in the academy.

Music, artificial fog, a spotlight—I can't even begin to describe it. Imagine New York, or imagine Paris—or if you're me, Moscow—but whatever you do, just don't imagine East Styria. It seemed like Brenner's entire body had grown ears, every pore an ear—you've got to picture this for yourself—and so the music was getting inside of him everywhere.

"Why so glum? You look like you just flunked your GED."

Suddenly, a redhead was standing beside Brenner—didn't even see her come in. He was still miles away in his head and remembering how once, on the force, they'd sat an entire night on standby and not a single call came in. They played Mau-Mau till four in the morning, a schilling a point, when all of a sudden, Oberascher goes out to the evidence room and comes back in with the cocaine they'd confiscated the day before.

And that's the dangerous thing about that fiendish stuff—years later, you'll often have some backlash like this, and out of nowhere, you're being dragged back into that trip, middle of broad daylight, even though you haven't taken any in years. And we even have a word for it here: flashback. English, you see, because that's how horrible it must be if nobody dares say it in German.

If there is such a thing! For Brenner it'd been, wait—thirteen, fourteen, no, fifteen years ago already, and now a flashback that practically had him clinging on by his toenails. And that's why at this moment he said to himself: "I think Löschenkohl fried my chicken in coke today."

But the whore must have understood it in spite of the deafening music, or she could read lips, I don't know. Anyway, she doubled over laughing, practically to her knees, and when she came back up, she giggled, "Chicken fried in cocaine! That's a good one! What's your name?"

She was still shuddering with laughter, but Brenner wasn't so dazed that he couldn't tell she was just waiting for an opportunity to jiggle.

Alas, she'd miscalculated. Because, exactly the opposite effect on Brenner. He smelled her pungent perfume, and it was over. Magic gone. All at once, sober as a stick again. You can have all the music and all the fog and all the flashbacks in the world, but when Brenner smelled that perfume, it was like flipping a switch. Suddenly, the chicken was coated in coarse breadcrumbs again.

"Simon's my name," Brenner said, because he thought, *why should I use a fake name, I'm old enough to use my real name at a brothel.*

"*Shy*mon!"

"Simon."

"No! *Shy*mon!" the whore shuddered with laughter again. "Because there's no need for a man to be *shy* in a brothel."

"So what's your name, then?" Brenner asked, because he was thinking: *if she's this talkative already, can't hurt, maybe I'll get led to the right one.*

"You Man! Me Angie!" Angie said. Because in every brothel there's an Angie, and this was the Angie from the Borderline in Bad Radkersburg. And when Brenner looked a little confused, she tried it again, the other way around.

"Me Angie!" she said and pointed at her breasts. Right, so she wasn't wearing anything, maybe I should've added that. And then she clutched at Brenner's chest and said, "You Man!"

Brenner had to buy Angie a peewee of sparkling wine, and even though he was making an effort to keep up his end of the conversation, after only her second sip she asked with great concern, "Why so glum? You look like you just flunked your GED."

And truly, if it weren't for the fact that this line of hers roiled him so much, Brenner might not have said just now, "How am I supposed to look when I see a pigsty like this?"

By pigsty, though, he didn't mean, in a moral sense, the brothel, but the table next to him. And I have to be fair here: everything else in the joint was *picobello*, meticulous, but the table right next to Brenner's, it honestly looked as though pigs had been rooting there. Broken glasses, bottles overturned, cigarette butts all over the table and the floor—the only thing missing was someone puking.

"Oh, that's just Palfinger," Angie said.

"Who's Palfinger?"

"Me Angie! You Man!"

This one's a real mallet, Brenner thought. And now he was actually glad that the music was as loud as it was so that he'd only have to understand half of her chatter. And these days if you only understand half of something, you can just as easily ignore the other half, too.

"That was a joke, like from Tarzan, get it? Me Tarzan, you Jane, get it: me Angie, you Man, get it? Which Tarzan do you like best? For me it'll always be Johnny Weissmüller. They just don't make men like him anymore. That's something I can vouch for."

Brenner was an expert at not hearing something he didn't want to. Because if you spend two decades in break rooms and police stations, then maybe you're an expert in narcotics, or a bit of an expert with homicide, or something of an expert in embezzlement. But you're only a complete and total expert at not listening. Because, day and night, your colleague at the next desk, and the secretary dealing with her divorce over the phone—who gets the parakeet and who only gets visitation rights when all is said and done. If you're not an expert at not-listening, you won't survive six months.

"Why so glum? You look like you just flunked your—That's him."

But the art of not listening, of course, is to listen again at just the right moment. That's why I say: expert. Because, easy enough for a person not to listen. But in the middle of complete not-listening, for a person to listen again at the decisive moment—that's what sets the specialist apart.

Brenner saw a fat colossus on rickety matchstick legs groping his way down the stairs. He clutched the banister anxiously, and even when he finally got to the bottom, Palfinger still needed half an eternity to make his way over to his pigsty. Then he flopped down onto the dark red armchair, causing a cloud of dust to rise, but the spotlight lent him a rosy aura of respectability.

"He even looks like a pig," Brenner yelled into Angie's ear.

"Shhhhhhh!"

Suddenly, it was Angie who looked like she'd just flunked her GED. "Are you out of your mind? That's our best customer."

"That swine there?"

Personally, I find fat people ten times more appealing than somebody who's just skin and bones. Because we've got people down here who are so thin, you'd think they got sent over in return for a donation to Biafra. One glimpse of this swine, though, and I have to say, you can't exactly get mad at Brenner for talking this way. Because it wasn't just his corpulence, but his entire way of being.

"That's Palfinger," Angie said.

"I don't know any Palfinger."

Angie didn't buy it at first. "Where'd you go to school?" she said, then knocked back the last sip of her sparkling wine and disappeared.

And when she came back freshly made up a minute later, she didn't sit down by Brenner anymore but by Palfinger, because she must get a higher commission there. But today just wasn't Angie's day, because before she could fully sit down, Palfinger booted her right in the can. And I've got to be honest—that Palfinger was so agile, well, I'm surprised, too.

The folks at the Borderline weren't surprised in the slightest, though, because they were used to his behavior. And even Angie was laughing, now that she'd recovered. And you see, that settled it for the whore: she simply sat back down beside Brenner and asked him if he'd buy her another peewee. But before Brenner could even give her an answer, Palfinger grunted over at her: "Get out of my spitting range, Angie."

And even though Angie cleared out instantaneously, it wasn't fast enough for Palfinger. From a distance of four, five meters—right in Angie's face.

When Angie was finally able to get back behind the bar, Brenner started looking around for another place to sit, too, because, no surprise, of course, he was thinking: *if I don't, I might be the pig's next target.* But before he'd even finished the thought, Palfinger was already way ahead of him. "There's a seat here at my table, bone-sniffer."

With something like this, there's always the old trick of acting like you didn't hear anything. And as far as your peace of mind goes, it remains one of the best options. How should I put it, though, maybe peace of mind wasn't what Brenner was necessarily looking for just now when he said, "What, can't hit a target twice from that distance?"

"Well, no need for a man to be shy in a brothel, bone-sniffer. It's like mountain climbing, once you reach two thousand meters, anything goes, and that's true for cathouses, too. Come, join me, and I'll tell you something. I never spit twice in one day. On principle."

"You can just as easily tell me that something of yours from where you're sitting now. A little distance never hurt."

Palfinger struggled like a person who's old and seriously ill, and it took him a few minutes before he'd finally freed himself of the low armchair and was standing on his matchstick legs.

Then, he slowly walked to the door in the back and called Jacky in. And it was now that Brenner saw that Jacky hadn't been too far off about his idealism. Because his real money was tied up in something else.

When Palfinger came back with some fresh grass, he sat down next to Brenner and extended his hand to him, perfect etiquette. "Allow me: Julius Palfinger. Please do me the honor of smoking with me. Jacky's finest harvest."

He talks about as stilted as he moves, Brenner thought. *The man's almost more unpleasant when he's friendly than when he's kicking your ass.*

"I don't smoke."

"No vices?" Palfinger smiled to himself.

Brenner was amazed by how quickly Palfinger's fat fingers could roll a joint. He lit it with an overlong match, like you'd use to light the pilot on a gas stove. After his first drag, Brenner thought, *now he'll get on with whatever his important story is.* But then, a second drag, and then, holding the smoke as long as possible in his lungs, and only then did Palfinger say, "May I ask whether in the course of your investigation you've come across any trace of my friend Horvath who's disappeared?"

It's an ironclad rule. People who claim they have something to tell you in truth only want to pump you for information. And those who act like they just have a quick question always want to tell you god knows what.

"You mean the artist, Horvath?"

"To others perhaps, he's the Artist, Horvath. To me, he's my friend Horvath."

"And who is it exactly that he's the Artist Horvath to?" Brenner asked. Because, as a detective, you're not there to let other people ask the questions.

"To his gallerist, he's the artist. And to the art collectors. And above all, to Marko."

"He's no friend to them?"

"Do you cash in on your friend when he hasn't even been missing a whole year?"

"Seems that way."

"Herr Gallerist Haselsteiner and Herr Art Collector Marko couldn't possibly have anticipated that they'd be the ones who would end up orchestrating the Great Horvath Sell-out."

"So, you're not on good terms with the two of them," Brenner said.

"Name me an artist who's on good terms with his gallerist and his largest collector."

"So you're an artist, too."

"Julius Palfinger," he introduced himself for a second time to Brenner and shook his hand again. But this time he added, "Austrian National Prize for Fine Art. Peggy Guggenheim Museum, Tate Gallery, Biennale, Documenta. Munich, Berlin, Zürich."

"Munich, Berlin, Zürich?" Brenner said. "I know those from playing DKT."

And true, in fact, there was a brief time when they didn't play Mau Mau on the nightshift, but DKT. *Das Kaufmännische Talent*, where you buy up properties and houses and hotels. But a game of DKT simply lasts too long when you've always got assignments coming in on the side. And so it just as quickly fell out of favor, and they picked up the Mau Mau cards again.

"So?" Palfinger said, startling Brenner out of his thoughts, "have you heard anything about my friend Horvath?"

"First, I need to find the woman who hired me."

"And what's with Ortovic?"

Brenner only shrugged his shoulders and asked Palfinger, "Do you know his girlfriend, Helene Jurasic?"

"I know every whore in Austria."

Don't follow up. Palfinger stubbed out his joint so meticulously, you'd have thought he was trying to win the Olympic medal in precision engineering. And then he said, "If I tell you where Jurasic is, then you'll tell me where Horvath is?"

"Okay."

Normally, Brenner never would've said "okay," and right there you could tell that he was lying. Because at that moment he still didn't have the slightest clue where Horvath was. He didn't even have the makings of a suspicion—for all he knew, the bones found at Löschenkohl's could have been Horvath's.

"Helene disappeared up to Vienna," Palfinger said.

"How do you know that?"

"I know every whore in Austria."

Palfinger's friendliness was beginning to fade again now. "And where's Horvath?"

"Dead."

Brenner only said that because he was afraid if he admitted that he didn't know, Palfinger might've gone totally Rambazamba again.

And actually, it was probably for the best. Because Palfinger remained very quiet—the only conversation he struck up over the next few hours was with Jacky's finest harvest. Until three-thirty, when the music stopped. Because maybe you're familiar with how quiet it gets when early in the morning the music suddenly gets turned off at a bar. And that was the moment when Palfinger's soft voice could be heard again, "Happiness and grass: both'll come back to bite you in the ass."

He only said it softly to himself. But Brenner could still hear it from three tables away. Even though he was in the middle of discussing the topic of flunking with a colleague of Angie's.

CHAPTER 7

Maybe the whole story would have turned out differently if the next day Brenner had driven to Vienna and looked for Ortovic's girlfriend. It's four hours to Vienna, though, and Brenner thought to himself, *Graz is on the way, and so I'll take advantage of an opportunity.*

Graz isn't even an hour away from Klöch. Nevertheless, a different world. And one thing you can't forget. Brenner was from Puntigam—practically a suburb of Graz—where the beer comes from, Puntigamer. You'd like to think this might take him back, you know, memories and all. Because he hadn't been to Graz since his father's funeral, and that must have been, unbelievable, six years ago.

But nothing, no sentimentality, where you might say: a childhood experience here, or a movie theater there, me and a girl for the first time here, and I fell off my moped once over there. Because Brenner had had a souped-up moped. When Brenner was applying to become a cop, they almost didn't take him on account of his record.

Then, nineteen years, police, and barely ever in Graz. Because he'd let them transfer him a few times, early on when his motto was: I want to see something of the world while I'm still young. Eisenstadt, Salzburg, Linz, Landeck, Attnang—he was everywhere, just not in Graz.

And now, all of the sudden, back in Graz, a certain sentimental impulse would've been understandable. Where you think to yourself, *I was so young, I had such high hopes, and now, it's just a matter of time before I'm wearing the wooden pajamas.* Because that was a saying on the force. But you'd have to ask a psychologist about it, and I'd be curious to know whether it still means something today for a person to call a casket "the wooden pajamas."

And it's that type of man exactly who tends to be sentimental. But Brenner was anything but sentimental now. He was just glad to have that fried chicken joint and that Klöch behind him. And Graz with its 300,000 inhabitants, Brenner breathed a sigh of relief—you just don't breathe that easily in Manhattan.

Now, why do I say "Manhattan"? You can't forget that Brenner had the impossible habit of whistling. And when he was a kid in Puntigam, hanging around his grandfather's carpentry workshop, *Ö-Regional*'s requests and dedications show played on the radio the whole time. I'm not going to apologize for Brenner's taste in music, though. And only time will tell if what's on the radio today is any better than "Die Rittersleut," which Brenner was now whistling to himself unawares.

There, now it's out. "Die Rittersleut," deepest depths of the beer hall, no way around it, it has to be said. But you can't forget, Brenner only knew one stanza of the song, listen up:

> "In Manhattan once lived an old knight
> whose cock got clocked off in a fight."

This should tell you how much everything in Klöch was weighing on him, the chicken, the staff quarters, the bone-grinder. And Ortovic's head turning up instead of Löschenkohl's daughter-in-law. And all of a sudden Brenner felt—and I don't mean for this to sound somehow, you know—like somebody was practically clamping down on his lifeblood. Picture a garden hose, then somebody steps on it, and no more water can go through. And it was only in Graz that the heavy shoe finally lifted.

Now he was making his way through thousands of shoppers in the pedestrian mall and whistling "Die Rittersleut." And sure enough, all that about the change of scene was only half-true. Because now he was starting to feel like he was in Manhattan a little: the crowds in the pedestrian mall, the countless signs for businesses that he passed, and how people just need to spend all of their money the first Saturday of the month—it all just felt so right to him at this moment. Although Brenner was usually a real spendthrift, and he'd often wear a pair of shoes until his toes poked through.

Maybe this only occurred to him now because he'd arrived in front of the shoe store he was looking for. It belonged to the sister of Löschenkohl's missing daughter-in-law, and as Brenner looked through the display window, he wasn't just whistling, he was even singing softly to himself.

"In Manhattan once lived an old knight
  whose cock got clocked off in a fight."

Maybe it was the springtime, too. Or he'd acquired a bit of a taste, let's say, at the Borderline last night. And that's why he was singing this song. I'm no psychologist, I don't know. But one thing I do have to say. The woman who he saw through the display window, well, she'd get any man to thinking.

Brenner waited there in front of the store until there weren't any more customers inside. But just like a jinx, whenever one customer would finish up, another one would go striding into the shop. Quite good for the saleswoman, of course, but not good for the detective.

Through the display window, Brenner was struck by how much the shoe seller resembled the Löschenkohl's proprietress. Löschenkohl junior had given him two photos of his missing wife. And ever since, Brenner had been asking himself just one thing: *how could a woman as attractive as her get the idea of marrying into a chicken dynasty?* Because you would've guessed just about anywhere—Paris, or over there where they've got all the swimming pools. Klöch, though. Anyhow, Brenner could understand perfectly well why the woman would run off.

And now the sister. When Brenner walked into the shop, he had to consciously restrain himself from whistling. And not that old-time whistling, maybe you still recall, where men would whistle after women on the street.

No, not to whistle his song. Because one glance at that woman had him silently whistling "Knight of Manhattan" to himself. Needless to say, something had stirred in Brenner, a feeling, and he was utterly relieved: *I'm still a man.* Because a mid-life crisis is a given these days when you're forty-five and stuck tying one on in Klöch.

"Can I help you with something?"

Now for some help. Brenner knew exactly what he needed help with. But he also knew what that would entail, which is why all he said now was, "Your sister's husband, Herr Löschen-kohl—"

The sister's contemptuous smile got under Brenner's skin—don't even ask. But he bravely continued—"told me I might be able to find—"

"She's not here."

"No, not your sister. You."

"Me?"

"I'm a private detective. Brenner."

"Aha."

Aha. Very interesting. A second ago Brenner was still being cocky, now his confidence was sinking away, as if into one of those deep bogs, where one minute you're up to your neck, and the next, of course, *arrivederci*.

"Herr Löschenkohl said your sister would often turn to you."

"Mmhmm."

"You don't happen to know where she is?"

"Can I help you with something?"

She was so stunningly friendly now, and when I said confidence and bog just now, then I must have meant: if Brenner's up to his neck, then his only hope is in that mop of hair of his.

And to that I should add: Brenner's confidence was unfortunately wearing a wig. And try pulling someone out of a bog by their wig sometime. You could really philosophize over that one, of course. But I'll just say it straight, even though it pains me to do so: Brenner smiled back gratefully. And when he looked into her eyes, he was struck by how, forty years ago, the main road that runs through Puntigam had been asphalted over. Because never before in his life had he seen something so glistening black as the fresh tar that they paved that street with.

And then Brenner realized. The look and the friendly question weren't intended for him but for the customer who'd walked into the shoe store just after him. And believe it or not, it was the woman from TV who does the daily weather in Styria. But Brenner only had eyes for the shoe seller, who had long, dark-red hair and black tar-eyes, in other words, a rarity.

And that truly was a coincidence, because Angie had had red hair, too, and the weather woman, also red hair. And there just aren't that many redheads. But that's how it goes—then you'll only meet brunettes for an entire year, and then only blondes—life's got a sense of humor all its own.

By the time the weather woman left, the saleswoman was so accustomed to acting friendly that, in the same tone of voice, she said to Brenner, "Could you maybe come by this evening? There's too much going on here."

"Gladly. Should I come by at six?"

"If that works for you."

Yes. Thank you. Good-bye. Brenner was happy. Now he could start all over again with the woman. *And besides, she's really quite nice*, he was thinking to himself now. *And besides, now I can walk around for a few hours.* Good weather, beautiful city—suddenly he saw his life in a completely different light. Just because the woman smiled at him. Men are such fools.

When Brenner returned to the shoe store at five to six, the door was already locked. And just as it was hitting him that shops close at five the first Saturday of the month, a black-haired woman said to him, "I had to get a quick dye job."

You see, red hair, black eyes, doesn't add up, this should've occurred to Brenner.

"Was the barber working overtime?"

Because Brenner was thinking, *best not to show any surprise.* Wrong time for games, though, and the shoe seller got right down to business without mincing a single word.

"How long has my sister been missing?"

"A week and a half."

"And so he got a detective right away?"

"Actually it was your sister who called me."

"Mmhmm."

Mmhmm. Never had Brenner dreamed that a shoe seller would give him goosebumps. But you should know, when he was a kid there was nothing he liked better than watching old Westerns, especially the Winnetou movies. And with her black hair, the shoe seller looked so much like the Apache knight's sister—if he hadn't known for a fact that Nscho-tschi died in Winnetou's very arms, he would've believed she was standing here in the flesh before him.

"Your sister called me a week ago. I was supposed to look into the matter with the bones. But when I got to Klöch, she wasn't there."

"I'm just surprised she didn't take off sooner."

"This isn't the first time she's left," Brenner said.

"No, but I always knew about it before."

"She'd come to you, then?"

"After a week at most, she'd go back again. To her chicken paradise."

"You don't think all that much of your sister's husband."

"What husband?"

Mmhmm. The arrogance of this Nscho-tschi shoe seller was disarming. And these days, of course, it's never good when a detective lets himself be so easily disarmed.

"Are you actually twin sisters?"

"I'm five years younger."

Now, thank god, a good excuse: "The photos I have of your sister are probably old."

Nscho-tschi only gave him a fake look, though, as if to say: *you think I need a compliment?* "The photos are fine. That's how she looks. In photos we always look very much alike. But in person, not at all. I don't know how that works, either."

"Just a way about you."

"Yeah, probably just a way."

Yeah, the older sister must have a nice way, Brenner thought.

"Why was your sister always leaving Klöch, then?"

"And here I've been asking myself why she always went back."

"For love, maybe."

"Or pity."

"For who?"

"How should I know. For the chickens, probably."

"Or the old man?" Brenner asked, and he was surprised when suddenly she answered in all seriousness,

"Could be. My sister felt sorry for the old man with his damn war injury. And the crazy ways he tries to make up for it."

"What kind of ways?"

"Maybe you think it's normal to grill a thousand chickens every day? And then every year having to put another addition on the restaurant because it's not enough for him? It's in the overcompensating that it becomes very clear just how perverse men are."

Back to the topic at hand, Brenner said, "And you have no idea where your sister could be?"

"If I think of anything, I'll call you. Where can you be reached?"

"Klöch. Staff's quarters."

"Aha. Well, good night."

Well, good night. It was only now when Brenner was alone again that he was struck by how deserted the pedestrian mall had become. The more he paced up and down the street, the clearer it became to him that he wasn't actually getting a single step farther.

"In Manhattan once lived an old knight
whose cock got clocked off in a fight."

Now, Brenner was quite happy that he still had a night in Graz ahead of him. Even though all day long he'd been a little apprehensive about it. Because Löschenkohl's daughter-in-law's sister was only of secondary interest for going to Graz. Of primary interest, needless to say: the Horvath exhibit that Palfinger had told him about.

Brenner had only been to an art opening once in his life. The wife of Salzburg's chief of police did needlepoint, Dutch windmills, and she couldn't bear to part with her works, but, a charitable cause. Because otherwise, just her husband's dark past always being dredged up in the newspapers for her windmills to do battle against.

But an art opening, a *Vernissage* in the proper sense of the word, with expensive works of art, this was Brenner's first time. The Horvath opening didn't go all that differently than the chief of police's salon, though. Because back then, all the young cops were busy kissing the chief's ass—so much so that the next business day saw Vaseline shares skyrocketing. And here in the Haselsteiner Gallery it looked just about the same, as if everyone had only come to pay court to one man.

This man was the exact opposite of the chief of police, though. Because the chief of police, of course, tall as a tree, wiry build, snow-white hair—you might've thought, freshly imported from Argentina. And here in the the Haselsteiner Gallery, a nondescript, forty-year-old man at most, who was so small that you might've thought, so this is why starving artists are all hunchbacks, because they're constantly having to bend down over him.

But I don't wish to be unfair now—there weren't only hunchbacks here—no, I should add: Brenner had never before seen so many beautiful and elegant people together in one place as he saw here in the Haselsteiner Gallery. And believe it or not, the most beautiful and elegant of them all first struck Brenner by the way he held his wineglass in front of his nose:

"How do you find Horvath?" Kaspar Krennek asked and pressed the wineglass into Brenner's hand.

"I'm not looking for him."

Somehow this answer reminded Kaspar Krennek of his father, the self-opinionated, post-War Hamlet, August Krennek. Needless to say, he didn't tell Brenner this. Because that was perhaps a topic for the therapist next Tuesday, not for an art opening. And now he just smiled and said, "I've already closed on it."

"You've got Horvath?"

"Two, in fact. The pencil drawing over there. And an etching in the other room. Because today I was able to stay in the bidding. In a month, though, the large sculptures that cost a fortune will be sold."

"But you've got to watch out. Because a Horvath can disappear—just like that," Brenner said and tasted the wine. But compared to the wine at the chief of police's, this was pure hooch.

"It's not exactly detrimental to the works that Horvath's disappeared," Kaspar Krennek laughed. "Before, I could've gotten my two prints for a tenth of the price."

"That ought to make the collectors who've been buying them all along happy."

"One collector above all," Kaspar Krennek said. "The rubber manufacturer, Marko, has bought a couple million's worth of Horvath's works over the last few years. And in a month, he'll sell them."

"For ten times as much?"

"If they don't go up even more."

Brenner noticed that Kaspar Krennek kept looking over at the small nondescript man. But the man must have noticed it, too, because now he was excusing himself from his young onlookers and coming over to Krennek.

"May I introduce," Kaspar Krennek said quite formally, because his good upbringing was getting the better of him again, "Nikolaus Marko, Austria's most significant art collector today. My colleague, Herr Brenner."

So my job as a private detective seems so lousy to him that he introduces me as a colleague, to be on the polite side, Brenner thought. But then he moved on to other thoughts. Because Marko was saying to Kaspar Krennek, "It's tragic how it's always the case that a dead artist is worth more than a living one."

"I've got to pat myself on the back," Kaspar Krennek smiled. "Just today, I, too, bought my first two Horvath prints. Ten times the price is but a fair penalty."

"A good purchase nevertheless," Marko congratulated him. "There's a lot of imagination in Horvath's works. And you're now in the fortunate position of being able to contribute something yourself. Your colleagues on the court are still making it difficult for us to get an official death certificate before the big exhibition next month."

"Maybe he's not dead at all," Brenner said, meddling.

Art collector Marko looked at him, surprised, and said, "I pray you're right. But I'd wager you're wrong."

"Praying and wagering," Kaspar Krennek said, imitating Marko's smile. The collector's speech had been so slurred that the two words sounded practically the same.

"Praying and wagering."

With each and every word, the Detective Inspector imagined the post-War Hamlet rolling over in his grave.

CHAPTER 8

From Graz to Vienna, it'll take you an hour and a half by car. But by train, nearly three hours. Because via the Semmering pass—that's the famous mountain railway—well, the architect of it used to be on the old twenty-schilling bill: Freiherr Ritter von Ghegha. Make a note of it, never hurts.

A hundred years ago, of course, technical tour de force—don't even ask. But nowadays, the one thing you notice above all else is how slow the train is. And Brenner was already feeling impatient because he'd gotten held up by the never-ending Horvath business. The time had come for him to find out: what's with the girlfriend of the beheaded Ortovic?

In his impatience, he'd set a pace for himself that he could scarcely keep up with anymore. BAM! find a conductor on the train who would sell him a prepaid phone card. BAM! find the onboard phone and look up the number for the Vienna PD's Vice Squad. BAM! request to be connected with Squad Head Winkler.

And didn't lose his cool about that thing with Winkler's wife—but I'm not going to go into that just now. Because it was fifteen years ago that Brenner had done that. And Winkler had been practically divorced anyway.

Didn't lose his cool, though. When the police operator picked up, normally that alone would've been enough for Brenner to catch a whiff of the police barracks again. Because nineteen years on the force, you don't just forget overnight.

Nineteen years of post-War furnishings, all of it first-class military quality, and nothing ever broke. At most, a fresh coat of paint when a suspect deliberately injured himself during an interrogation. Or, let's say, his nerves sent him puking higher up on the wall than a coat of paint could reach, so it'd needed to be whitewashed out. And the phone system had been updated, and computers, too, of course, but still the same old typewriters. Because for some documents, typewriters—simply irreplaceable.

The lamps, the laminate flooring, the bulletin boards, the desks, the coffee makers, usually all it took was a surly "Police Precinct Two" and there'd be that smell. Usually! But Brenner—like a changed man now. He got redirected three times, he even heard background noise, but he didn't let in any of the funk.

"Hofrat Winkler."

"Hofrat, eh? Congrats on the promotion."

"What promotion? Who is this?"

"Brenner. The last time we saw each other, you were still an inspector. And I was, too."

"Ah, Brenner, I almost didn't recognize you there. Didn't think I'd be hearing from you again."

Winkler was always good-natured. His wife walked all over him, it wasn't even funny anymore. She looked like that actress in the French film—real quick, what's it called again, the one they reran on TV recently.

Winkler didn't let anything show, though. Who knows,

maybe he'd completely forgotten about it. Men are all very different. And Winkler had always been an uncomplicated type. It'd been an eternity, too. Anyway, where am I going with this: two minutes later Brenner had Jurasic's address. And shortly after noon, he was already standing at the Praterstern roundabout.

When Brenner was a kid in Puntigam, he would always listen to "Hit the Road" on the radio while he had lunch. It was really a very good program. Robert Stolz and Peter Alexander and call-ins and tips and everything. And every day at noon they would broadcast the midday bells from a different place in Austria. Except Puntigam never got featured, supposedly a slight because someone came forward with a sex scandal involving the town priest.

So Brenner knew the Praterstern from the traffic reports long before he ever set foot in Vienna for the first time. Interesting, though! Even though Brenner had only ever heard it mentioned when there was a traffic jam or construction or an accident in one of the traffic circle's six lanes in the middle of downtown, he always imagined the Praterstern roundabout as something beautiful, almost a different planet. And it must've been that way for Helene Jurasic too, for her to name her Praterstern bar the Milky Way, of all things.

When the train let Brenner off directly on the Praterstern, first thing he did was walk over to the police trailer. Because he was feeling a little lost in the middle of the roundabout, which was supposed to be his starting point to look for the Milky Way bar. So, out of old habit perhaps, straight over to the police, this should've been a clue. Basically, they'd put this trailer there—you've definitely seen these at construction sites, the trailer where the masons go to drink at nine in the morning. No masons here, though, just police.

And once he was standing at the police trailer, he could see for himself that across the street next to the Nissan dealer, the red lights of a bar were blinking. Now he just had to cross the four, five, six lanes of traffic, direction Nissan dealer.

When Brenner got to the Nissan dealer, he was still alive, that's the good news. The bad news, though: the bar wasn't Helene Jurasic's Milky Way. So he continued walking around the Praterstern: from the Nissan dealer, he crossed the Heine-straße to the Hansy Restaurant, crossed the Praterstraße, then the underpass at the Franzensbrückenstraße, then the metro underpass, Hauptalle, nothing, Ausstellungsstraße, nothing. Lassallestraße, nothing.

He saw it all: the Admiral Tegetthoff Monument, the Ja-maica Sun Solarium, the Ferris wheel, the Avanti gas station, a fast-food place, and if he'd walked down the side streets, too, he would've even found some other bars: Rosi, Susi, the Black Cat. After forty-five minutes he was standing right back in front of the Nissan dealer, but not a Milky Way in sight.

Now, you really don't want to be caught walking around the Praterstern for long. Because maybe there's a brutal mur-derer afoot in Klöch, but what's one murderer when you've got the whole Praterstern. And you can't forget what bad drivers the Viennese are. Paris, not good, either. Nairobi, also not good. But Vienna—terrible. And when you've got six lanes of the worst drivers in the world driving around your ears, you can lose your cool pretty easily.

But it wasn't the honking and braking and screeching that tugged on his nerves as he was making his second lap around.

No, it was the white Mercedes that came out of nowhere, rumbling right up onto the sidewalk and narrowly grazing Brenner's toes.

Now, who's that sitting there gloating in his white Mercedes, you're probably wondering.

"Hey, Brenner, what brings you to Vienna?" Vice Squad Head Winkler asked innocently.

He must have remembered that fifteen-year-old story with his wife after all.

"Very funny, Milky Way," Brenner said.

"What, you're looking for the Milk Way?" Winkler grinned. "You're in the wrong place. This is just a roundabout. It doesn't go anywhere near the Milk Way. It's just a simple traffic circle down here on Earth."

"You don't say."

Brenner was still as pale as a sheet. Because, first of all, a beer in the dining car on the train that morning, which he's not used to. And then an hour and a half circling the Praterstern. And then going under the wheels of Frau Winkler's husband's Mercedes.

Brenner must've been feeling a little weak in the knees. That's the only explanation I can come up with for why he took Winkler up on his offer. Because he held the car door open to him and Brenner, knowing no pride, got in.

"No hard feelings, Brenner. It was just a joke."

"Very funny."

"That was always your motto, Brenner."

"Yeah, yeah. Long time no see."

"Get this: didn't miss you at all."

Winkler had put on at least thirty kilos since they'd last

seen each other. But Brenner didn't say anything. He was glad to be sitting in a comfortable Mercedes and glad to be chauffeured out of the Praterstern.

"Jurasic, Helene, lives in Red Heights," Winkler said.

"Milky Way. Red Heights. You must be going through menopause, making up things like that."

"Good to see you can still take a joke. Milky Way's a good one."

"And Red Heights?"

"Do you know anyone who lives in Red Heights?"

"Sure. Rudolph Schock. I used to always watch him on TV back in Puntigam."

"I forgot you're from Puntigam. Then you can't know what it means to live in Red Heights here in Vienna."

"Yeah, yeah. Puntigam: a miracle I even know my own name."

"You didn't used to be so sensitive, Brenner."

"Where exactly are we driving?"

"To Red Heights."

Alas, when two old dopes get going like this, it often ends up with both of them losing their bearings. Because Brenner knew for a fact, of course, that Red Heights was the hill where the overstuffed Viennese keep their houses. And he could tell that Winkler wanted to help him, after he'd laid into him about the Milky Way. But no, Brenner was being stubborn now and just didn't want to hear anything else.

First, he had to digest his defeat by way of the Ruckzuck method. At some point in your life, you have to pull yourself together via the Ruckzuck method and chalk it up to a flub that Winkler managed to trick you. And he'd never been one of the brightest. But, now Brenner was thinking: *best way to find out what Winkler wants to tell me is to keep mum.*

But watch closely. It wasn't really a long enough drive for the silent treatment. Winkler was already driving deep into the enclave of villas atop the hill that was Red Heights—with every meter the convertibles got more and more expensive, with every garden the Rottweilers got more and more nervous, and with every house the automatic firing systems got more and more sensitive.

Brenner didn't allow his fat chauffeur to get the upper hand, though, and showed only the slightest bit of surprise when Winkler let it slip that the Radkersburg Yugo-whore Helene Jurasic resided here, among the bank directors and ministers.

But when they arrived at her villa, his jaw dropped. Not because of the villa, even though it was a proper Jugendstil or what have you. And not because of the garden, even though it was an immense park. And not because of the two Rottweilers, even though they tried with all their might to squeeze themselves through the wrought iron gate.

But because parked in front of the house was a silver Porsche, gleaming peacefully in the sun.

Maybe it only looked peaceful compared to the two Rottweilers behind the garden fence, though. Brenner walked past the silver Porsche and, without asking any questions, opened the garden gate. Now why would he have no respect for the dogs, when one look at Brenner sent saliva running down their chops?

And that's where Winkler comes in. Because he's still sitting in his police Mercedes, grinning, and waiting to see whether Brenner has the balls or not. And needless to say, Winkler was already looking forward to seeing the man who'd been such a hero in his wife's eyes get—pardon my German—torn a new one by the Rottweilers.

As Brenner opened the gate, he felt Winkler's gaze at his back, and the Jurasic Rottweilers' gaze at his feet. Now, they say dogs can smell fear. And that's when they get really aggressive. Because that must be, for a dog, like when a person, like you or me, walks by a bakery and becomes ravenous just from the smell.

Now, Brenner had opened the gate so quickly, on account of Winkler, that he hadn't had any time to get scared. And maybe that's why the Rottweilers didn't tear him into a thousand pieces. Even though it was right about snack time.

At the last possible moment, though, fear must have entered into it after all. Brenner was giving off an irresistible bakery scent. Because when he was almost to the door of the house, one of the two Rottweilers went flying through the air all of a sudden, like a black snowball, or if you picture those iron wrecking balls that they tear down old houses with. Because the builder thinks, first I'll drive the wrecking ball in, and then I'll conjure up an apartment building, marble everything, gilded fixtures and all that, and then I'll rake the money off to the side, and then I'll go bankrupt. You see, that's why there are so many new apartment buildings in between the villas of Red Heights.

Jurasic's villa, though, hers was a real jewel box. And that's just on the inside! Because now Brenner was standing inside, in Helene Jurasic's villa. Because he hadn't exactly found the time to knock.

"Do you not keep your doors locked?" he said, when the lady of the house came out of her bedroom.

"Pardon me?"

"You. Door. No lock?"

"Most people are respectable," Jurasic, Helene, said in ex-actingly high German. And gave Brenner a cheeky look as if to say: *first of all, what are you looking for in my house? And second, spare me your pidgin German.* On both counts, Brenner felt he was innocent, because it was the Rottweilers that were guilty of the first, and Milovanovic of the second.

"You'll have to excuse me for barging in like this, but the dogs."

"You were barging in on the dogs as well."

Brenner wasn't going to be able to talk himself out of this one as easily as he might have with Winkler. So he was quiet, because Jurasic was too quick-witted for him anyway. And someone's got to say it: he belonged ever so slightly to that category of men who get easily intimidated around a quick-witted woman.

She made an immediately intelligent impression on Brenner. But maybe he also belonged to that category of men who think that any woman with short hair and glasses makes an intelligent impression. I can only say this much: on TV game shows when they cheerfully guess your profession, they'd never guess Helene's, because she didn't look like a whore—typical hand gestures aside.

He wouldn't have placed her at more than eighteen years old. Then again, he himself was already of an age where you underestimate the age of all young people. Because Helene was petite and lithe, but she'd celebrated her thirtieth birthday last

October. Which, in zodiac terms, made her a Libra, but I don't
believe in all that, although—Helene was trying to appease
him just now, and so you could say, typical Libra, balancing
the scale.

"What are you looking for, then?"

"A friend of yours lost his head."

"The police already found it."

"It's the rest of him I'm interested in."

"You'd be better off asking him," Jurasic said, unmoved, and
led Brenner into her living room, where Löschenkohl junior
was sitting. He looking rather desperate, he cried out:

"That would suit the Yugo-mafia just fine, pinning Ortovic's murder on my shoulders. But I know I'm going to find
Milovanovic here. Even if I have to sit here all night."

Two minutes later, Löschenkohl junior was standing right
back out in front of Jurasic's jewel box. With Brenner next to
him. The two Rottweilers, very well behaved now—they obey
that wisp of a woman, heel, incredible. And you see, that's
why I don't like dogs, one minute they're practically tearing your head off, and the next they're pandering to you—if
that's what you're looking for, you might as well just stick with
people.

Now, Brenner didn't get anything out of Jurasic, Helene.
Because Brenner was her third visitor that day. And she hadn't
told Kaspar Krennek anything about her dead ex-boyfriend
and Milovanovic, the missing goalkeeper, either. And he at
least had known how to behave himself. But anyhow, Brenner
was able to get a ride back with Löschenkohl. Just a pity that
he'd bought a round-trip ticket for the train.

He got to Klöch three times faster, though. Because, these

days, if you drive 190, nonstop, then you only need an hour to go 190 kilometers. For forty-five minutes, Löschenkohl junior didn't say a word. Was it a coincidence or not, though, that as they were zipping by a chicken plant, of all places, that had recently gone bankrupt, Junior began talking?

"Six months ago, Ortovic went to the newspapers and claimed that I had bribed him on the elimination game between Feldbach and Klöch. It was a bunch of lies. I couldn't figure out what he'd get out of slandering me. I was trying to find something out about him back there. A few weeks ago, I got the idea that I could find something about him in the old Yugoslav sports pages. Because, common knowledge, he used to be a big deal in Yugoslavia."

"Like Milovanovic," Brenner said.

"I can't read the Yugoslav papers, of course. But I found a student in Vienna who went to the library and skimmed through the papers for me. She copied and translated those places where Ortovic's name appears. I picked up the translations from her this morning," Löschenkohl junior said, pulling a couple of folded pages out of his sports coat and handing them to Brenner.

Then, Brenner read that it was Ortovic who had stomped on goalkeeper Milovanovic's head.

"Now I understand why you're looking for Milovanovic. But I still don't understand what Ortovic gets out of slandering you."

When you're driving from Vienna to Klöch on the autobahn, you have to exit at Ilz. Then you can take either the western route via Feldbach or the eastern route via Fürstenfeld. Fürstenfeld's nicer, and then you can take the Wine Road down to Klöch. But via Feldbach and Riegersburg, it's a little faster. And those fifteen kilometers between Ilz and Riegersburg, Löschenkohl junior vacuumed them right up in his Porsche—Brenner swallowed in Ilz, and by the time they hit Riegersburg, the spit wasn't even all the way down yet.

And then, on the way from Riegersburg to Feldbach, Löschenkohl junior said: "I don't know, either. I only know that my wife disappeared at practically the same time Milovanovic did. And that Ortovic's head turned up that same week."

The church in Feldbach had a modern steeple made out of concrete. It used to be gray, but then they got a young priest— he'd even been a hippie at one time—the gray concrete steeple didn't appeal to him. So he'd had it painted, top to bottom, with bright splotches of color. And because the hills aren't any higher, you can see the steeple from far away, long before you get to Feldbach. Of course, when you zip by as fast as Löschenkohl junior, though, you only see it for a few seconds.

"Did you see that house of Helene Jurasic's? What do you think a bungalow like that costs in Red Heights?"

Löschenkohl junior pronounced it with an "a," as in "bangalow." There have always been two schools on this: the one says it with a "u" and the other with an "a," and maybe that's the reason the word's fallen out of fashion.

It even seemed to Brenner now that he hadn't heard it since his aunt in Puntigam had taken part in a bungalow contest. She'd only won a yellow plastic weeble, though, and she'd given it to Brenner. But memories like these can whip through your head at a speed that a Porsche can't possibly match. And immediately Brenner answered, "Fifty thousand a month she's shelling out."

Then, Löschenkohl junior's arrogant laughter again. A mixture of condescension and "Please don't hit me." A dangerous mixture, Brenner thought—although if that's the way it is, then nearly every one of us must be dangerous.

And Löschenkohl junior was looking more pitiful than fearsome now. In a car, you see the other person pretty close up. So Brenner could see that his fat neck was so sweaty and covered in flaking skin that involuntarily he thought: *no hair—but dandruff in spite of it—that's just cruel.*

"Jurasic, Helene, doesn't pay a single schilling a month for her house," Löschenkohl junior said.

"If you've got the right friends."

"Helene Jurasic doesn't have any friends anymore. But she has a twenty-million-schilling house in Red Heights. It belongs to her—I looked it up in the land register."

"What sort of bank lends that kind of money?"

"No mortgage."

I kind of think it bugged Brenner a little that Löschenkohl junior was playing detective all on his own—and not too clumsily, either. At any rate, he said somewhat sarcastically, "Really quite useful, a register like that, where you can just go and look everything up."

"And to think that just a few weeks ago, she was still down here with us, climbing into any car for three hundred schillings."

They were just passing Bad Gleichenberg. Then, it was over to St. Anna, and at ten to six, the Porsche was parked in front of the chicken joint in Klöch.

Brenner didn't even have the opportunity to thank him for the ride, because within a moment of Brenner getting out of the car, Löschenkohl junior was already speeding off. Just a Brenner delivery, but no interest in seeing his father.

That morning, Brenner had taken off for Vienna full of optimism. Out into the world. And now it had snapped him straight back to Klöch like a rubber band. One thing I'll say: Brenner wasn't the hysterical type, I know him at least that well. But now, at ten to six, this dump on the Slovenian border was nearly making him hysterical.

Now, when you're close to hysteria, it's best if you eat something. Brenner ordered himself a Cordon bleu, and then went up to his room.

Maybe you're familiar with this: it's too early to go to sleep, but you also don't know what to do with the evening. That's what old man Löschenkohl had put a small TV in Brenner's room for. But TV wasn't the right thing now, either. A VCR would've been good right about now, and not just any old VCR, but the kind where you can fast-forward your own life a full day ahead.

He must have fallen asleep in his clothes because at ten-thirty he was startled awake.

I'd prefer not to say what startled him, trust me on this. It had to do with you-know. Intimacy. And what it comes down to is—it's nobody's business but your own. And everybody should do as they please.

The waitress must have had a needlepoint sign hanging over her bed that said: "Work Before Play." Because she worked a lot, Brenner could see that every day. A good waitress, you've got to admit, with strong arms for schlepping beer steins.

And about the play, what should I say. He could hear it again now, just like he did every night. But today it seemed even louder to him, maybe only because he'd just been asleep. Brenner was just amazed that the waitress managed to find so many lovers. Because one thing's got to be said in all honesty. A beauty she was not. Nice, yes, competent, yes, pretty, no. No need to discuss.

And when, punctually at eleven-thirty, he overheard her lusty cries, Brenner thought: *and now I'd like to know what kind of lover the waitress has taken up to her room tonight.*

Now, this is something you can only know if you've slept in the staff's quarters at an inn before. That they often—unique to old country inns—only have thin wood partitions. It was once an attic, and now it's the staff quarters. And so you see all over again how important it is for a detective to have a good pocket knife with a corkscrew. Because with a corkscrew you can drill a small hole into a wooden wall that thin, just like so.

I don't know, was it just curiosity that had Brenner thinking, *and now I'd like to know who exactly this lover is?* Or, what with the Porsche snapping him back to his room so fast, was it the shock from reentry into Klöch? Either way, he had to do something to get himself thinking about other things.

Or was it a certain sexual, you know, after all. Like the little boys who like to peek over at the other side of the changing rooms at the swimming pool. You'll laugh, but there are wunderkinds who can't swim an inch, but who could take over the Chair of Gynecology in an instant.

But when Brenner saw Horvath on the other side, he grabbed his pistol and hopped on over to his neighbor's room.

CHAPTER 9

When Brenner woke up the next morning, at first he thought, *a dream,* of course. Because when human beings don't want to know something, first they hope it's a dream. But no, it was no dream that he had found Horvath in the waitress's room.

Brenner remained very calm, though, and thought to himself, *I just won't let on. First, I need a little more information about Horvath before I can take any action.*

He knew that both Marko and Palfinger had farmhouses in St. Martin, and before he'd even had breakfast, he was down at the stop waiting for the nine o'clock mail truck to St. Martin. He stood on the side of the road for an eternity before he finally saw the truck off in the distance. As the green mail truck slowly crept down through the green hills—a spectacle of nature, just wonderful, I've got to say. But Brenner, needless to say, somewhere else in his thoughts.

He didn't get much out of the drive, either, he was so pre-occupied with Horvath. It could have been a wonderful drive in the nearly empty nine o'clock mail truck. I certainly don't want to come across as patriotic, or as the saying goes: no place like your own home. But I've gotten around a little in my life, too, last year, Egypt, convenient arrangements, and at the breakfast buffet—you can take as much as you want! And the pyramids, of course, stunning sight, nothing like it.

But driving through Styria in an empty mail truck, as Brenner now was, remains some of the greatest beauty that you can experience in this world: the sun, the fields, the vineyards, and the one-story toy farmhouses, any one of which could have won a floral decorating contest. And don't even bother about the suicide rate again, because suicide rates are everywhere, but floral decorating contests? Not everywhere.

Once in St. Martin, Brenner was on the lookout for the most beautiful farmhouse, and on the mailbox, needless to say: Marko. After the fourth ring, though, still nobody had answered. Now: *should I ring a fifth time, or should I knock, or should I shout, or should I give up?*

Before Brenner could even decide, Palfinger came out of the neighboring farmhouse. Brenner almost didn't recognize him. At first he thought, *it must be the sunlight that's making this ravaged swine from the Borderline look civilized all of a sudden.* But it wasn't the sunlight, no, it was as if the whole Palfinger package had been traded in. Polite and quiet, sure, but also not like he was trying to deny that he knew Brenner from the brothel. Because men are often strange about that kind of thing, and the next day they don't want to know you anymore.

But Palfinger didn't have any problem with that, he came right over to Brenner and said, "Marko's disappeared."

And Horvath's turned back up, Brenner thought. But, needless to say: best to keep it under wraps.

"Yesterday he invited me for dinner. Because Marko likes to cook," Palfinger said.

"Did he make anything good?"

Now, Brenner was a little casual there. At the Borderline, he'd been stiff where everyone else had been casual, and now he's casual all of a sudden. Brenner's just a little peculiar sometimes.

"Didn't make anything—because he wasn't there," Palfinger said. "He made a big show of saying that he'd make me blood sausage because they'd slaughtered a pig at Neuhold's in Klöch, and Marko promised me he'd bring back the blood and make fresh blood sausage."

"That was yesterday?"

"He came over around noon, quite hungover from the opening. And blood sausage is the best cure for a hangover. He took off right away for Neuhold's. I worked hard all day and really worked up an appetite. Because blood sausage is only good when you're hungry."

"And when it's hot," Brenner said, because he thought, *what applies to frankfurters must be double for blood sausage.*

"But then, there I was, just standing there with my appetite, in front of Marko's closed door. I called Neuhold's, but Neuhold was also wondering why Marko hadn't shown up. Because Marko's car was still parked in Klöch, but no trace of him."

"He'll turn up again," Brenner said, because it was getting to be a little too much for him right about now, how fast people were disappearing down here.

"Sure he will. Do come in, though. I was just cooking."

"Just now?"

"Cooking's what I do."

"Cooking and painting?"

"Painting, less so. But cooking."

"What's cooking today?"

Brenner was amazed by how clean and tidy Palfinger's kitchen was.

"Today I'm making Klachl soup. Do you care for it?"

"I'm not fussy."

"You can't be fussy when it comes to Klachl soup," the painter laughed and took two big bones out of a pot.

"So, those bones are for the soup?"

"Pig bones. Not from a human. Human bones aren't good for anything."

"Not for soup."

"Not for soup and not for anything else, either. I know someone who's broken twenty-three bones."

"Car accident?"

"Just little things. Fell out of bed, down a rib. Took a wrong step, the ankle. Slipped in the bathtub—"

"Bathtub's dangerous."

"Yes—fractured the base of his skull."

"It just defeats the purpose. Freshly showered, blood running out of his ears."

Now, you should have seen Palfinger. The blood was running out of him, too. Not out of his ears, though, out of his face, which was white as a wall.

An artist like this is a difficult person, Brenner thought. *On the one hand, a real roughneck, then again, extremely sensitive.* And only a moment later did Brenner understand why Palfinger had reacted so sensitively all of a sudden. Because he himself was the man with the broken bones. The man who had fractured the base of his skull. And to be frank, no surprise at all, given how overweight he was.

"Something like that can only occur to an artist who talks about himself in the third person."

Palfinger didn't say anything to that. He didn't say anything at all for a spell, just busied himself purposefully with his Klachl soup until a little of his color returned.

"You probably don't have enough calcium in your bones," Brenner said.

"You think that's why a person falls over in the bathtub?"

"A skull fracture, though?"

"Skull fracture's not the worst."

"So what's the worst?"

Palfinger didn't answer, but instead said, "I had the bloodied bathtub torn out, and I put it in an exhibit."

"And what did you call your work?"

"'Smashed Skull.'"

"So you exaggerated."

"I always exaggerate everything. I rode a bike so fast that I did a somersault."

"And did you put the bike in an exhibit?"

"Don't bullshit about what you don't understand," the painter said, suddenly as touchy again as he'd been that whole night at the Borderline. Because he never would have put the bike in an exhibit, but try explaining that to Brenner—why the bathtub got turned into art but the bike got repaired.

But the painter wanted to explain something else altogether to Brenner now.

"I can't move properly. I limp once with my left leg, and once with my right. Because I don't have any rhythm. Every day I bump my head at least once. Do you understand?"

"What's there to understand?"

"That's why I like to cook. Because when I'm cooking, I'm at peace. I never burn myself cooking. I never drop anything. And not once have I hit my head while cooking."

"Even though you've got everything hanging over the stove."

"My body gets very warm when I cook. My thoughts get quiet. And sometimes I'm so at one with cooking that I wish I could cook myself."

"Now you're exaggerating again."

It seemed to Brenner like Palfinger wasn't listening anymore. And as a matter of fact, he didn't say a word for the next fifteen minutes, just acted as if Brenner wasn't even there. This was a contrast—a few days ago, totally berserk at the Borderline, and now so quiet and even-tempered while cooking that Brenner wouldn't have been surprised if the halo that the spotlight at the Borderline cast on Palfinger should suddenly reappear. Even though "halo" is a bit of an exaggeration because I don't think there's much cooking being done up there—they'd have to borrow some fire from their rivals down below.

Brenner was starting to brood a little because he couldn't imagine why Marko would disappear—and now, of all times, when he'd just found Horvath. He wasn't getting anywhere, and it was raising a doubt in his mind again about whether this was the right profession for him.

So, he was glad when Palfinger finally ladled up the Klachl soup. Because a bowl of hot soup is always the best cure for a depressive mood, it should really be covered by insurance everywhere today. It warms the soul—it's not for nothing that that's how the expression goes. And after a few spoonfuls, Brenner was feeling like himself again, and right away, a concrete question like you'd expect from a detective nowadays.

"Does Marko live here in the farmhouse all year?"

"Half the time he's in Graz. Apart from yesterday, the last time I saw him was a good week ago. He'd had quite an argument with Jacky—I could hear it from over here. Jacky probably wanted his money."

"Marko was a customer of Jacky's, too?"

"Everyone's a customer of Jacky's. But Marko's shortcoming was that he never paid. And Jacky wasn't the only one he ran up debts with. He'd buy my paintings but never pay me for them. Invite you for blood sausage but never give you the money."

"It's always the same with rich people. I just wonder whether it's the millionaires who are all tight-fisted or whether it's the misers who all become millionaires."

"Don't make me laugh. Marko, a millionaire. Horvath was his last hope."

And now, Brenner's technique for sounding someone out: don't follow up. And this time it worked. Because Palfinger filled both their bowls again, and then he said, "Do you even know how Marko made his millions?"

Even though the soup was making Brenner so hot that sweat was streaming down his forehead, he started in with his spoon again right away, i.e. I eat, you talk.

"Tires," Palfinger said.

Brenner now: "Can you really earn that much off tires?"

"If they're bulletproof, and if a war breaks out a few kilometers away, where bulletproof tires are needed for the vehicles, then, sure. That first year of the war, Marko was raking it in like a fool. Most of us artists profited from it. The prices of paintings skyrocketed. Because a big collector in a small country—he can drive prices up. And Marko bought everything that he could find."

Brenner drew his head down a little and continued spooning up the soup, well behaved. And Palfinger kept talking, well behaved.

"But when the boycott on imports went into effect, Marko was left sitting on his pile of tires. And this enormous factory with two hundred employees. That'll eat up your fortune pretty quickly. By the time Marko was getting rid of his collection, the price of paintings had hit rock bottom, too. He only held on to a few artists."

"You and Horvath, for example."

"Except, then, the rumor sprang up that Horvath was dead and prices skyrocketed again. That saved Marko."

"So his only hope is that Horvath doesn't turn back up."

"At least not before the big exhibition next month. With the sculptures. Because this week they started with the prints. But Horvath's really a sculptor."

"How close friends are you and Horvath, really?"

"Horvath was a loner. He didn't let anyone get close. And you couldn't get him to eat with you, either. He was the best cook I've ever known."

It seemed a little strange to Brenner that these artists were all so crazy about cooking. And he would have liked to ask Palfinger how that happens. But he knew that on no account could he say anything now, and so he let Palfinger keep talking.

"Horvath had a sense of taste that I would best compare to having perfect pitch. You could season something with twenty-five spices, and after the first bite, he'd have listed them all off.

And he didn't cook like a cook, but like an alchemist in his laboratory."

"What a bunch of crap."

Shit, that slipped out of Brenner. He'd just never been able to stand it when the better folks talked about cooking. This whole nouveau riche pretense, how they examine the wine with a thermometer first before they drink it. Maybe he was only sensitive to it because it always managed to remind him of the certified interpreter he'd once schlepped to Florence, and after two days, they were fighting so much that they had to travel home separately.

But it didn't bother Palfinger one bit that this had slipped out of Brenner.

"A bunch of crap," he nodded, "That's how it must have seemed to Horvath, too. He suffered from compulsive eating. Eating, puking, eating, puking, eating, puking."

"Usually only women do that."

Brenner tried to say that as casually as possible. Maybe too casually. Because Palfinger didn't say anything in response.

Maybe he hadn't really heard it. Or didn't want to hear it. Or honestly didn't know that, for nearly a full year now, Horvath had been working at the Löschenkohl Grill as a waitress, and night after night, serving as his own lover.

CHAPTER 10

Real quick now. Brenner got a ride back with the noon mail truck, and somehow he managed not to puke it full up to the parcel rack. Not because of the Klachl soup but on account of this one little thing that Palfinger had told him.

Because, given how incensed he'd been about Horvath's delicate sense of taste, Brenner only had a few seconds to press for the truth. And then, it dawned on him. And then, he had to ask himself why the waitress had only been eating sausages for months on end but avoided the fried specialities of the house like the plague. And then he had to go and connect that observation with this question: the human bones found at Löschenkohl's—where exactly did the flesh end up?

And at the very thought that he himself might have in-gested one of these fried bits of flesh, well, it stretched Brenner so far that the half-hour ride on the mail truck seemed about as long to him as his entire life up until now.

When he got back to Klöch, it was peak business time at Löschenkohl's. Hence, down to the basement to see Jacky's mother, who'd just finished mopping the hallway.

"Where's Jacky?"

The bathroom attendant was always so cheerful that it got Brenner to thinking: *you see, this is good for a depressive mood—if you have to be preoccupied with the negative*. Philosophy, as it were: one person's interested only in fashion and trifles, but secretly he's depressed, but the bathroom attendant—who has to clean up after everybody else—pure sunshine.

No sunshine today, though, no—eyes puffy from crying and a trembling voice: "Gone."

Brenner waited, but that was her entire answer.

"What happened, then?"

The bathroom attendant didn't utter a word.

And then, I can't explain it any other way—she must have felt ashamed all of a sudden. Because she turned around and disappeared into the women's bathroom.

Needless to say, an awkward situation for Brenner. On the one hand: *should I follow her?* On the other: *as a man nowadays, you don't just go into the women's bathroom without batting an eye.* But when the bathroom attendant didn't come back out after a few minutes, and because there was nobody around just then, for the second time in his life, Brenner went into the women's bathroom.

Because there was this one time in Lofer when he'd had to collect a suicide from the women's bathroom at Café Moser. He could still remember how the kitchen was right next to the bathrooms and the whole time he could hear the chef's radio. And when he pulled the suicide's ID from her wallet, at that very moment, Udo Jürgens was singing from the kitchen, "Siebzehn Jahr, blondes Haar." And believe it or not, the dead girl, also seventeen with blond hair, just like the song.

Now that Brenner was in the women's bathroom at Löschenkohl's, he didn't see the bathroom attendant. With fifteen stalls, though, needless to say, she could be anywhere.

"Frau Trummer!" he called, but no response. "Frau Trummer, say something please!"

Frau Trummer didn't say anything, though. He didn't hear a peep out of her. So Brenner looked to see whether any of the stalls were locked because—you know how it is with restaurant bathrooms, depending on whether a red or green status indicator is visible on the lock, you know right away: Vacant or In Use. A good invention actually, for once somebody came up with something. All the stalls were empty, though, Vacant indicators everywhere. So Brenner started opening the doors, one after the other.

When he was already on the second-to-last door, Frau Trummer—still nowhere. And then the last door, not only no Frau Trummer but not even a toilet inside. Only an empty stall. And no tiles on the wall either, just another door.

Brenner knocked, and he could hear Frau Trummer's sobs from behind the door now. Brenner still thought it was a broom closet that she was hiding in, and so he opened the door slowly.

But then Brenner was in for a surprise. Because it wasn't the door to the broom closet that he'd opened. It was the door to Frau Trummer's apartment. She not only spent her entire day working in the bathroom. She lived in the bathroom, too. She was sitting there on her old rust-brown divan in her ten-square-meter hole in the wall that only got a little bit of light from her two basement windows.

Now, Brenner was momentarily a bit speechless when he saw old lady Trummer sitting there in her basement hole with her head in her hands.

But maybe a person shouldn't be so thoughtless as to call

another person's apartment a hole. And even if it was only ten square meters and practically dark even in the light of day and toilet smells and sounds inside—to Frau Trummer, it was still her apartment. And so a person doesn't need to come down here and condescendingly call it a hole, just because chance has treated a few other people a little bit better than this. Because there are people who own entire houses, and from the rooftop terrace you can see all the way to Africa. And despite this they still have a hole—in their heads—and that's what I think about that!

Frau Trummer had appointed her apartment as nicely as possible: a small credenza, beige, like those poor people in the fifties used to have—well, these days it's back in style. A rust-brown wicker divan, something as comfortable as this you just don't find anymore today. A kitchen table with a starched white tablecloth, and over the tablecloth, a clear plastic runner. Which is appreciated if you spill something, because then you can just wipe it up like it's nothing, and the tablecloth beneath stays *picobello*.

"So what happened?" Brenner asked, but Frau Trummer just shook her head.

He simply sat down on the white kitchen chair now and waited.

And after a few minutes, Frau Trummer said, "My boy's disappeared."

"How long's he been gone?"

"A week," Frau Trummer said. "That's not it, though. Three days ago it was my sixtieth birthday. He promised that he'd take me to Graz, to the Emperor of China. And he'd never forget something like that. Even as a little boy—always kept his promises. He said I have to try Chinese food just once because I've never had Chinese." Frau Trummer pulled out a large handkerchief from beneath the divan cushion. "I don't need any Chinese food. And I don't need Graz. But, my son I need, because otherwise I have nothing."

And then she blew her nose, but it was pointless, because she started crying again right away.

Brenner didn't get much else out of Jacky's mother. And when he saw on her old porcelain kitchen clock that it was almost two-thirty, he had to get back upstairs to catch the waitress. Because at this point there wouldn't be any more customers, but the waitress wouldn't be on break yet, either, so this was the best opportunity.

And if you're going to be a detective in this day and age, you simply can't let yourself be guided by sympathy. Sure, he liked the waitress—I like her, too, I freely admit. And on his way up to the dining room, he was still secretly holding on to one hope: *if, one by one, everyone's disappearing, maybe in the meantime, the waitress has already disappeared, too, and I'll get out of doing this.*

But the waitress, of course, there as ever. Not to mention the fact that she was sitting there with a schnapps. Completely alone, middle of the afternoon. And Brenner had never seen her drink anything but coffee.

"I could use a schnapps right about now, too," he said and took a seat at her table.

"You got that right," the waitress said, tossing the rest of her schnapps back, and walked over to the bar. She didn't have to stagger so much, though—Brenner could already tell from the way she'd slurred her words that this wasn't her first schnapps.

But you can take a competent waitress off her shift, but you can't take the competency out of the waitress, and a few seconds later she was back with Brenner's order.

Except she hadn't brought a schnapps, not even two, but the whole bottle.

"This is the home brew. For staff only."

"Am I staff now?"

"You sleep in the staff's quarters, don't you?"

"When you look at it that way, all right."

"Whoever sleeps in the staff's quarters is staff, so be it. And whoever doesn't sleep in the staff's quarters doesn't get any moonshine."

"Does Löschenkohl distill it himself?"

"Löschenkohl? He brews Blitz at best."

Now, though. You don't need to be a detective to be able to tell that the waitress had a problem. Even someone like you or me would've been able to tell right away. Because no one had ever seen her so vulgar before—on the contrary, a lovely woman. Competent waitress, lovely woman. And now something like this.

"This is Klaushofer's home brew."

Brenner didn't say anything to that, he simply took a sip of the schnapps that the waitress had poured him. And I don't want to alarm you now but—then he had another gulletful. There was a moment, though, when Brenner thought: *over and out—and only intravenously from this point forward.*

"Eighty-three percent, Klaushofer's fruit mash."

"You need a firearms permit for this."

"But it doesn't do anything to you," the waitress said. "Because it's such pure schnapps, only apples in it."

"The apples might not do anything. But that percentage will."

"Where, though? It doesn't affect you at all," the waitress said, and filled both schnapps glasses again.

"I could use it anyway," Brenner said and reached for the freshly filled schnapps glass.

"It doesn't hurt one bit."

And down went the second schnapps. Interesting, though, the second burned far less than the first. Needless to say, the third—only apples and they don't do you any harm.

"People are very distinctive when they're intoxicated," the waitress said.

"Very distinctive? Very different, you mean," Brenner said, because alcohol always makes him need to be right a little.

"Yeah, different. Anyway. But, distinctively different!"

"Mmhmm," Brenner said, "distinctively different."

And thought to himself, *now I've gone and said "mmhmm" just as arrogantly as that Nscho-tschi in Graz.*

"One person's fun, another gets aggressive. And another turns sentimental and squeezes out a few tears."

"And others lecture," Brenner said, because he was thinking, *why am I letting myself get lectured by a fake chicken waitress instead of taking her to task?*

And whether there's telepathy or not, I don't know, but it was at that moment exactly that the waitress told him something that would prove revealing for Brenner. "There was a call for you earlier."

"From who?"

"Here's the number," the waitress said and slid a beer coaster at him that she'd written the number on.

"Whose is it?"

"I forget. You can call back, you know."

"Vienna area code," Brenner said.

"*Oje*," the waitress said.

"What does '*oje*' mean?"

"*Oje* means shit."

"What do you have against Vienna?"

"Nothing, I don't have anything against frankfurters, either. As long as they're hot! Debrecener's are good, too. I have absolutely nothing against sausage."

"Except your own."

You see, you often put off something uncomfortable for days before you say it out loud. And then when you do, it's crass and clumsy.

On the other hand, though, why would you want to make something like that sound elegant, and so maybe it's better that the schnapps was helping Brenner out a bit.

"I think we're both feeling the schnapps."

That was the waitress who said that. Don't be mad at me, but I can't bring myself to say "Horvath" all of a sudden. Even if, in the end, it was Horvath who filled the schnapps glasses back up again.

"*Prost*, Brenner."

"But don't get aggressive with me," Brenner said.

"Me aggressive? Schnapps makes me fun, mostly," the waitress said, and in the same instant, began to cry. "So now it's out," she said softly.

And Brenner said, "Now it's out."

And the waitress drank her schnapps and wiped her mouth

and said, "Now it's out." And then didn't say anything for a while. And then she said, "Now it's out. And now you think that I have something to do with the bones in the basement."

And Brenner said, "Not necessarily."

And the waitress said, "A man posing as a woman, something must be wrong with him."

"Not necessarily," Brenner said.

"Not necessarily. Except bones are turning up in the restaurant where he works," the waitress said and got up. "I'm going on my break now."

And then Brenner was left sitting there alone with the schnapps bottle.

But he didn't pour himself any more schnapps. He sat there and ruminated. Well, more like brooded. Like when you're sitting in the sun and thinking about something. You think that you're thinking, but really you're brooding. And instead of the sun, it was the schnapps that warmed his belly.

If Brenner had been thinking, though, then it probably would've been about whether the waitress, i.e. Horvath, was the Bone Man or not. What speaks in favor of this, and what speaks against it? And what sort of motive could there be, he might've thought about. And why Löschenkohl's daughter-in-law? Why Marko? Why Jacky? Why Ortovic and Milovanovic? And who was that very first one they found? And if he'd been thinking, he might have finally brought his investigation into something resembling a line, instead of continuing to stumble aimlessly through East Styria.

But he didn't think. And maybe all these questions occurred to him while brooding, too, but needless to say, a terrible mess. And maybe, simultaneously, he was brooding over his left shoe, why he always got a hole in the same place, left shoe, pinky toe. With new shoes, too, it's the same exact thing.

Because that's the advantage that brooding has over thinking. That you can brood over everything simultaneously. He brooded over the sounds coming from the kitchen every bit as much as the pictures on the wall calendar. Because with brooding, you can't choose what you're going to brood about. It's different than, say, thinking, where you have a bit of choice in the matter.

With brooding, you have no control over what comes out of it. Could be a huge surprise, let me tell you. Another thing that makes it different than thinking is that you can't dial the surprise down a little. A surprise is still possible with thinking, but it's not going to bowl you over, let's say.

I don't want to say anything against thinking, though. Because with brooding, less than nothing comes of it most of the time. You brood a little, then you fall asleep. That's the only surprise you experience in a normal case of brooding. Something startles you awake, and—surprise—you think, *I just fell soundly asleep.* And most of the time, we only brood because we're too lazy to think—that bears saying, too.

But now I'm starting to brood a little myself, so you see how easy it is to slip right into—it's jinxed!

But then Brenner really did get bowled over when he woke up from his brooding: shock, no other way to put it. But not because he'd been brooding over something so profound, a higher insight or something, where you might be able to say, you see, brooding paid off for once, and a good thing I'm too lazy to think.

No, Brenner was startled out of his brooding now because a strange man came in wearing the exact same shirt as one that Brenner owned. Now, the shirt alone could still be a coincidence. But, same pants and shoes, too. And needless to say, double-shock for Brenner, because on Horvath's feet, he saw for the first time in his life just how noticeable it really was that his left shoe had a small hole in the pinky toe.

"I don't have any men's clothes anymore."

"So my shoes fit you."

"I'm a forty-one. A little big for a woman."

"I'm a forty-two, a little small for a man."

It's from remarks like this one that you could tell that maybe Brenner had a bit of a complex when it came to his height. He's a completely average height. It's not his height that makes him look so compact, though. No, his shoulders are too broad and his legs too short, that's it, i.e. proportions.

"Better too big than too small," Horvath said.

"How did you get into my room?"

"Skeleton key. From the housekeeper."

"So you're not going as a waitress any more?"

"Going?"

Brenner would've been better off biting his tongue: going as a waitress! Like it's Halloween. I'm going as Charlie Chaplin because all I need's a black suit, a hat, and a mustache, and then I've got a good costume.

Horvath just smiled, though. He was nowhere near crying now. He also seemed completely sober when he said, "No, I'm not going as a waitress anymore."

"So, what do we do now?"

"Now we go for a little drive in my car."

Brenner left with this slim man who was wearing his checked shirt, which was way too big for him, and got into the waitress's Ford Fiesta.

The Ford was full of the kind of crap that certain people have in their cars, a CD was dangling from the rearview mirror, a crocheted toilet-paper-cover doll was standing on the rear shelf, and a "Get Home Safe" picture frame was glued next to the glove box. But the yellowing photo of the man in the frame must have been circa Elvis Presley, because the kiss curl—a catastrophe.

It didn't come as a particular surprise to Brenner that to-day's man can decide: I'd rather be a woman. And there are even operations, and he understood all that. And that an artist might think, *I'd like to be an ordinary person again*, he under-stood, too. But that someone would go so far in his transfor-mation as to have a crocheted toilet-paper-cover doll in his car—that was something Brenner couldn't comprehend. And was thinking to himself now, *maybe that's the reason why the waitress made such a racket every night. Maybe it wasn't purely lust. Maybe there was also some twinge of a desire to be caught, i.e. 'liberate me from my toilet-paper doll.'*

The schnapps and the drive were making Brenner so slug-gish that he nearly fell asleep. But he had to pull himself to-gether because he still didn't have a good hold on what to make of Horvath. And in a case like this, where it's your own bones at stake, falling asleep is never the ideal.

After a solid hour, they arrived at an old dilapidated farm-house that was set back from the road.

"This is where I grew up," Horvath said, after they'd both gotten out.

"Looks like nobody lives here now, though."

"Not for fifteen years. Since my father died."

A garage of sorts had been added onto the small farm-house, but merely a wooden frame, and no door—the way it used to be, in order to store the hay wagons. This barn, which Horvath led Brenner into, was twice as large as the entire farm-house. A few rusted tools still hung on the walls, where there were patches of moss and grass that had spread between the wooden beams over the years.

Because, needless to say, nature's merciless. At first, it was mankind that was merciless, building our way into nature, but turns out, nature's not so noble, either—the moment a person takes his eyes off things, everything's already grown over. They're really just two brutal forces coming together, and I don't feel sorry for either one of them.

When Horvath pushed open the rough wooden door along the back wall of the barn, Brenner first became aware that he'd been hearing the quiet rush of a stream this whole time. Just behind the back wall of the barn, a stream flowed past. The stone ramp between the stream and the barn wall was just wide enough for two sets of feet to stand side by side. Horvath closed the barn door behind them as they went to stand outside. The wild stream roared so loudly that Horvath had to shout for Brenner to be able to understand him. "When I was a kid, I'd always come out here whenever my father snapped!"

Brenner didn't say anything to this. First of all, he didn't want to shout, and second of all, a roaring stream like this is meditative. A stream like this you can stare right into like you can a fire—a person often does his best thinking that way. But

Brenner was thinking of one thing primarily right now: *in case Horvath's the murderer and he's about to shove me into this wild stream, then he will have pulled it off, and not too terribly.*

Horvath was still going on with his story, though, which he was shouting into Brenner's ear. "Outside here, no one could see me crying, or hear me, either, because the river's so loud. Except for once when I must have been crying so loudly that my father could hear it inside. He came out and saw me standing here. Then, he came over, raised his hand, and stroked my hair. It was so much worse, though, than the slap I'd been expecting him to give me."

Brenner had never been one to make very much of childhood stories like these. It was uncomfortable for him in the same way that going to a unisex sauna was. Or maybe it had nothing to do with the unisex sauna—no, listen to this.

He'd once had something to do with a woman, that would've been Kerstin. She always wanted to go to the sauna with him. And why not, good for the health, and the whole winter that he was with Kerstin, Brenner didn't catch one cold, because the sauna, goes without saying, great for that. And when it was over with Kerstin in July, of all months, Brenner got the flu, sweated a whole week long—sauna doesn't come close.

But maybe it was more of a psychological thing, where you might say, a breakup like that and all. And even if it only lasted for one winter, it's still a matter for the unconscious, and as soon as you're looking the other way, the virus gets you.

Grew apart, mainly, because Kerstin was a real chatterbox, always yammering on about her childhood and psychology. Brenner was in fact very interested in psychology, but for police reasons. Because psychology's very important on the force. But Kerstin and her childhood—and there she'd go again.

And you see, that's what I meant by brooding. Everything's a little messy, and when a person stares too long into a river, it only gets worse. Or maybe it was still the schnapps that Brenner had drunk earlier that made him useless at snapping himself out of his brooding. But he knew himself well enough to know that it was a good sign when he finally quit thinking. Because thinking had never been one of his strengths. But brooding, world class!

Horvath was standing like his back was glued to the barn wall. He talked a great deal, but the whole time, all Brenner heard was the stream. And it was only when Horvath went back inside that Brenner was torn away from his brooding.

Brenner followed him inside and watched as he opened a door that led from the barn into a workshop. From the road, only the small farmhouse could be seen, but behind the house was the workshop, and behind the workshop the barn, so everything was much bigger than a first glance would have you believe.

"My father was a cartwright, an obsolete craft today," Horvath said, opening the door, and now pay close attention to what I'm about to tell you.

At that moment when Brenner stepped inside the workshop, he was so terrified that his mind thought of something else altogether: back when they were just kids, they'd once broken open the door to the church tower in Puntigam and climbed all the way up into the bell cage. And there they'd found a pile of skulls, a few hundred skulls it must've been, delicately and neatly stacked, one on top of one the other.

Because it was a church custom to collect skulls, more so in the older days, and originally they'd been displayed at the entrance to the Puntigam church, as if to say: *remember, mortal, you're going to die.* But then, the murder reforms—so they opened a shop next to the entrance, postcards and all that. Now, where to with the skulls? The priest said, *you know what, we'll store them in the tower, they're not going to bother anybody there.*

Well, the boys were a little bothered, and they ran away so as not to get into trouble. And that must've been why it occurred to Brenner just now. That he'd much rather be running away, just like he'd done back then. Because when he entered the workshop, he immediately took in the five butcher blocks.

He was familiar with these, too, from even further back in his past. When the butchers didn't have the high-grade synthetics yet. They'd cut the meat on wooden tables—you need to picture it more like a square chopping block. Now, over the course of the years—the butchers chopping and chopping all the while—the surface of the wooden tables would grow uneven. Like water running over a stone for a thousand years. And, over time, hilly landscapes formed out of the butcher blocks.

And you see, Horvath had bought up all these butcher blocks and declared them his works of art. Because that's allowed in art these days, you can just go and pass off anything you find. That wouldn't have been allowed before, but nowadays, reforms everywhere, church reforms, and art reforms, too. Now the reforms allow Horvath's butcher blocks.

Other than the five butcher blocks, the only other thing in the workshop was an electric bandsaw that was so big, it practically hit the ceiling.

"When I was seventeen years old, I got my first boyfriend. He was nearly forty."

As the devil would have it, Udo Jürgens immediately sprang into Brenner's mind again. Because Horvath had blond hair, too, though more of a mousy blond.

"The photo in the Fiesta?" Brenner asked.

"We fell in love when I was thirteen. But, needless to say, impossible, so he went to Saudi Arabia for four years to work. Came back and then—really in love. But still impossible, of course. We would meet every night, right here in this workshop. Those people practically beat him to death when word of it got out. Somehow he managed to get away and hide out.

A few days later, he returned to the workshop. On a Sunday while we were all at church. He turned on the bandsaw. It made so much noise that the entire house shook. Terrible noise."

Horvath had to smile a little at his own mention of the noise, and then he said, "So he could prepare himself. Because you don't get into heaven when you slit your own throat."

Horvath had to smile a little again now when he saw Brenner's face. Then he continued, "As we were coming back from mass, we could hear the bandsaw running from far away."

Horvath walked over to the bandsaw now and reached for the black power switch on the back of it. Brenner instinctively ducked his neck a little out of fear of the noise. But the switch only made a *clack*.

"No power," Horvath said and laughed.

When later they wheeled Brenner into the intensive care unit, he could still hear Horvath's laughter in his unconscious.

CHAPTER 11

Nice and slowly now, one at a time.

By the time Brenner and Horvath climbed back into the Fiesta, it was already getting dark. Horvath drove through the twilight, and the two of them talked so much that you might have thought it was no regular Fiesta, but an especially strict Fiesta with a vow of silence.

Then, the Fiesta didn't take the turn-off for Klöch, but, no, the opposite direction.

"Heard anything from Marko?" Brenner asked.

"Why?"

"Because he's disappeared."

"He hasn't disappeared. I just saw him yesterday at the restaurant."

"What was he looking for there?"

"I'll give you three guesses. You know, you made him nervous, showing up at the opening like that."

"Why would that make him nervous?"

"Marko's facing bankruptcy. The banks are already on him about the rubber factory."

"Rubber's back in style now," Brenner said.

"That can't save Marko anymore, either. Not even enough rubber to make a rubber."

"I'm not talking about that kind of style," Brenner said. "I'm talking about rubber tires being in style down Yugo-ways."

"Then you know about the ban on imports, too. That he's stuck sitting on a pile of his own tires."

"I don't feel sorry for him," Brenner said. It struck him that Horvath and Palfinger presented their stories in the same exact way. But just because two people don't contradict each other doesn't mean that something hasn't been lied about. You've got to be careful not to over-analyze.

"I don't feel sorry for him, either. When things were going better for him, he bought up almost all of my work. He must have at least fifty butcher blocks."

"What did they cost him?"

"Twenty, thirty thousand schillings at the time. But ten times that since I disappeared."

"Two, three hundred thousand?"

"I've always thought you were good with numbers."

"Wanted to line his pockets with the millions from the butcher blocks."

"But then a little problem got in his way. You're not a cop anymore, so I can tell you. And it won't make a difference to Jacky, either."

"Do you think Jacky's dead?"

"I get that feeling. Although for him I do feel sorry. Not just because he's my dealer. But because, when I disappeared as Horvath because I finally wanted to be myself, I wasn't all that interested in grass anymore. Because it doesn't really go with being a chicken waitress, and I wanted to be a completely regular waitress. But then, when the stress picked up, first with the bones and then with Ortovic, I bought a little off of Jacky."

"To ease the stress," Brenner nodded.

"At first he was surprised that a waitress wanted to place an order with him. But when I gave him my order, he recognized me right away, of course. Because everyone's got their special order, a dealer can recognize you even in his sleep. But he didn't let on. I like Jacky for that. And a handsome man, too. But he's a stray mutt. Went straight to Marko and blackmailed him: said he'd let it slip that I was still alive—before the exhibit."

"Send prices plummeting, naturally."

"It occurred to me that I hadn't seen Jacky in some time. Yesterday, though, Marko shows up all of a sudden. He'd known where I was hiding for a few days already, thanks to Jacky. But when you showed up at the opening, he nearly lost it. He thought that I was behind the whole thing—that right before the big exhibition that was going to restore all his finances, I was going to let it all fly. He would've liked to beat me to death with his own hands—just so it would be true, finally, that I was dead. He started threatening me that he'd pin the murder on me, and started screaming like a lunatic: '*I know whose bones are in the basement. I know, and I'll testify if you turn up before the exhibition.*' He was completely beside himself. He practically ripped off my breasts. But, at that moment, the old man intervened and threw him out."

"So, whose bones are they?"

"You'd have to ask Marko."

They were driving into Bad Gleichenberg now, a sleepy resort town, where just driving through gives you the creeps. But they weren't just driving through, no—Horvath pulled into the parking lot of Little Joe's Disco.

"What are we doing here?" Brenner asked. He couldn't

quite make the whole story jibe, and he was so tired from trying that he could have fallen asleep right there on the spot. And going to a disco was the absolute last thing Brenner wanted to do right now.

"I'm driving back home. But you should go to Little Joe's," Horvath said and pointed at the silver Porsche that was parked out in front of the place.

"How'd you know that Pauli would be here?"

"Because he's here every day."

"Does he own the place?"

"Don't make me laugh."

"What's he doing here, then?"

"Where do you think his whiskey hangovers come from?"

It seemed strange to Brenner that Horvath felt such aggression toward Löschenkohl junior. You'd like to think that one low-life might have a little sympathy for another. But, needless to say, completely the other way around. Basically, it's the same exact thing with dogs. A poodle only needs to catch a glimpse of a smaller pinscher to get worked up into a savage frenzy. Whereas a Rottweiler is humanity personified.

"And ask him where that twenty million walked off to that was still in Löschenkohl's account a year ago. I know about it from his wife," Horvath yelled out the open Fiesta window.

Once in Little Joe's, though, Brenner was wide awake all over again. Because one thing you can't forget. Disco today isn't the same old disco. There's disco and there's disco. But a disco like the one in Gleichenberg you're not apt to find anywhere else. A disco architect really came up with something here. The entire disco was outfitted like a barn, you know those nests where the animals are penned up. And the feed troughs, the hoses for watering—it was all there.

The men were leaning against the troughs, bored, and watching the only three girls who were actually dancing. Because it's the same the whole world over, Bad Gleichenberg or Manhattan, doesn't matter: the women like to dance, the men prefer to watch like idiots.

When Brenner took the pig ramp up to the next floor, though, he was relieved. Upstairs, no barn, just a totally normal bar setup. He went right over to Paul Löschenkohl's table, and without even saying hello, Pauli asked him: "Found anything out yet?"

"Not directly."

"And indirectly?"

"Just like with a free kick," Brenner said.

Löschenkohl junior looked a little dim.

"And you never know which is more dangerous," Brenner said.

"So you like soccer?"

"I like the twenty million that Ortovic slandered you over with that bribery story of his."

Löschenkohl junior gestured to the waiter to bring him another round. Even though his whiskey glass was still almost full. His face was as bloated as if he hadn't been near anything else in years. When the waiter brought the fresh whiskey, Paul quickly threw back the one he had as though he was only doing it for the waiter's sake—a big help, as it were—so that he could clear the glass away.

Brenner didn't quite know what he should order, then he got a coke.

"Rum and coke?"

The server's hair glistened like it was smeared with chicken grease.

"Coke, no rum."

Because Brenner was just glad he wasn't feeling the schnapps from that afternoon anymore. Although he was just imagining things, of course, because you think you don't feel it anymore, but of course, you still feel it for some time after, it's been proven.

"You just want to bluff me."

Löschenkohl junior, Pronunciation Master of the World once again. Not just "bangalow" but "blaff" now, too—at least he was consistent. But then, as inconsistent as an old drunk again. Because he only fought it for a few seconds, and then he began.

He told his story very slowly. Slow as someone who's concentrating on every single word. But not what you're thinking: he was concentrating because he was lying. No, when you've been lying your whole life long, it overrides your flesh and blood. And then you have to concentrate when you're telling the truth.

"My father built his chicken place back in the forties, out of a small bar where the local wines used to be sold. When we were first starting out, we'd often only sell a few glasses of white wine. Hundred schillings, that was on a good day. Over time, though, better and better. Then we expanded, and even more people. And a few years later, expanded again. And then again. I don't know how often."

Paul had taken his beer coaster and was scribbling nervously on it with his pen.

"It wasn't long before my mother took off, because my father only had money on his mind. She married a Yugoslavian. My father didn't fully realize that she was even gone. And he expanded again. Eventually we had the feeling that, on any given weekend, we were feeding half of Styria."

This whole time, he didn't look at Brenner once, just kept scribbling on his beer coaster while he talked.

"Then I got married. My father liked my wife a great deal. She had business smarts, and soon, she'd taken over the finances. I became less and less interested in the business. My wife, less and less, too. It was my mistake, bringing her into the restaurant. The more she had to do with the chickens, the less interested I was in her."

On the red beer coaster were white letters that spelled out: LITTLE JOE'S DISCO, BAD GLEICHENBERG. And Paul was slowly making the word LITTLE disappear with his red pen.

"Nevertheless, she came to me this one time with a problem. Father had spent a million schillings in a single week. She said I should talk to him. But he didn't want to hear anything about it. Over the next few months he spent five million. I followed him once and saw that he'd been going to a prostitute."

In the meantime, Paul had colored over the next word on the beer coaster, too, so that only DISCO BAD GLEICHENBERG remained.

"You know that my father hasn't been a real man ever since the war. That's why, just a few years after it ended, he married my mother, because she already had a child. She left me with him so that I'd inherit something. And now, my father, who hasn't looked at a woman in fifty years, gives six million to a prostitute? I've followed him over and over again and he's only ever gone to see Jurasic, Helene, Ortovic's girl-friend."

Now only BAD GLEICHENBERG was still legible on the coaster.

"Then, ten million were gone. My wife said, 'That's half of what he's earned in his entire life.' And I had to get him declared legally incompetent or else the entire business would be gone. So I went to the courthouse with all the documents that I needed to prove it, but in addition to the bank records, I needed at least one witness, too. Then, in the time it took me to track down a witness, another two million disappeared."

Only GLEICHENBERG was still gleaming white now on Paul's ever-reddening beer coaster.

"And then Ortovic found out that I was trying to get the old man declared legally incompetent. And he got the idea that he needed to get me declared incompetent before I could get my father legally declared. Well, a public declaration—made me look ridiculous so that no one would believe me. He came up with the bribery story. Making it impossible for me just about everywhere in Styria."

LEICHENBERG. When Paul was done with his story, he looked at Brenner inquiringly.

"And you expect me to believe your story?" Brenner said. Because although we know today that every last word of Paul's was true, at that moment, Brenner didn't want to believe him.

"You can ask Jurasic."

"Jurasic's in Vienna," Brenner said. And at that moment it crossed his mind that he still hadn't called the Vienna phone number that the waitress had written down for him.

"You can take my car."

Now, Brenner was anything but a car enthusiast. He didn't even have a car. But a little stroll in the silver Porsche? How should I put it? Who wouldn't have been tempted?

"You just have to watch out with the anti-theft device," Löschenkohl junior said and gave Brenner the key, as well as a keyless remote fob that would remove the steering-wheel lock at the press of a button.

And it was indeed at the press of a button that Brenner forced it open, but he wished that the damned iron thing could be stowed away at the press of a button, too. Because in a Porsche like this, there's not much space, and it was the biggest steering-wheel lock he'd ever seen.

Brenner just shook his head, because he knew for a fact that professional car thieves could have a thing like this open in a matter of seconds. Whether it's a little bigger or a little smaller, makes no difference: Freeze-It spray, hammer, open— and for all that, it takes ten times as long just to stow it. But then he wedged it behind the bucket seats on the diagonal, and that's how it went.

And you see, that's what I've been saying. Because, he didn't even want to drive to Jurasic's. He hadn't even called her yet. Brenner just wanted to take a lap in the Porsche. And people always say, the child inside the man, and make fun of him for it. But if Brenner hadn't taken the Porsche just now, then we'd have one more grave to visit at the Klöch cemetery today.

CHAPTER 12

I need more time to complete this sentence than Brenner did to take the Porsche from Klöch to Vienna and back. Because two hours past midnight found him lying back in his staff bed. Needless to say, though, no talk of sleep.

These days, if you knock off four hundred kilometers on the autobahn in a silver Porsche—silver streak on the horizon, as it were—then you should just be glad adrenaline isn't coming out of your ears. But adrenaline wasn't the least of the reasons for why Brenner couldn't fall asleep.

Because I'm not even done with this sentence yet, and Brenner's already done with Helene Jurasic. This time she wasn't playing around, and she told Brenner exactly how she got old man Löschenkohl's fortune out of him. And in such detail that Brenner regretted not having drunk a whiskey, or at least a rum and coke, back at Little Joe's.

As he lay in bed now, he could still see the taillights of cars on the autobahn, flickering through the darkness. The red dots approached so quickly that he sometimes thought the taillights were mounted on the front, i.e. oncoming traffic.

Brenner stared up at the wood-paneled ceiling, rubbing the tip of his left middle finger against his left thumb over and over again. You know, like when you have a blister someplace and you can't stop touching it. Except, now imagine someone popping open a blister he got from flashing his headlights so frequently over a few hundred kilometers of autobahn—also a minor world record.

It was three-thirty already, but he had to keep going back over again and again what Helene Jurasic had told him a few hours ago. And he could feel how nice and slowly the headache was creeping up from behind his collarbone. Because, first comes intoxication, then the headache—basis for a whole philosophy.

Brenner, though, not so philosophical now. Because, these days, a headache's exactly the wrong thing to have with difficult thoughts. It's like turning on the Turbo in a headache-Porsche, and so the headache enters from those tense neck muscles behind the left ear, and a few seconds later, you don't know how you're supposed to see straight anymore.

Needless to say, Brenner wasn't going to make a dumb mistake like that now. Because he had something perfectly easy to think about. Really, is there anything easier than thinking the same thing over and over again? And Brenner was thinking again and again about how it had been Goalkeeper Milovanovic who opened the door at Helene Jurasic's. And what Milovanovic and Jurasic then proceeded to tell him.

But I need more time to finish this sentence than Brenner did to grasp who the Bone Man was.

Four o'clock in the morning now, and Brenner still wasn't asleep. And then, finally, the headache arrived. He tossed and turned, from one side to the other, and it seemed to him that the squeal of the bone-grinder was only getting louder.

And then he had to think about Helene Jurasic yet again. And then about Milovanovic. And then about Löschenkohl junior, who'd loaned him his Porsche. And then about the waitress. And then about old man Löschenkohl. And then, for the fifth or sixth time already this night, he got up. And saw that it was still pitch-black outside. And then he made himself earplugs out of toilet paper so that he wouldn't have to hear the squeal of the bone-grinder.

And then he thought, *why should the bone-grinder even be squealing day and night anyway?* And then he thought—because when you're lying awake at night, you often think of every possible thing, things that would never occur to you during the day—*now that Milovanovic hasn't run the bone-grinder in nearly two weeks, how tall the mounds of bones must be that are piling up around the basement.*

And then he didn't stuff the toilet-paper plugs into his ears. He got so curious all of a sudden about what it must look like down in the bone cellar that he got dressed and went downstairs to the bone cellar.

He thought, *better not turn any lights on in the hall, you never know what good that'll do.* And he noticed that, in the dark, sounds are much louder. And the sound of the bone-grinder was getting louder with every step that Brenner took in the direction of the bone chamber. And then, of course, huge surprise.

Because the door to the bone chamber was locked. That wasn't the surprise, though, no—there was no noise coming from behind the door. No squealing, no nothing.

Now where did the squealing disappear to? If I can hear the bone-grinder up in my room, but I can't hear it down here, how many possible explanations are there? Either, someone turned the machine off while I was coming down here. And this someone is perhaps waiting behind a curtain for me, with a butcher knife. But here in the basement, not a curtain in sight.

Or, the squeal that I've been hearing from my room this whole time hasn't been the bone-grinder at all.

Then, Brenner heard the squealing again. But from the opposite direction. And then he searched for where the squeal was coming from.

He walked back down the hall, but the squealing was everywhere and nowhere. He thought about whether he should wake up the bathroom attendant and ask her where the squealing came from. But, yesterday, out of concern for her son, the bathroom attendant had gone to her sister's in Bad Reichenhall.

The bathroom attendant's gone, and her son's gone, and the waitress is gone, Brenner thought, while in the half-dark he listened at the different doors in the basement. He even listened at every door of every single bathroom stall, and listened especially, of course, at the door to the bathroom stall that disguised the bathroom attendant's apartment. And then he opened the stall door and listened at the apartment door. And tried the apartment door to see if it was open.

But, naturally, the apartment was locked. And then, Brenner forced it open. And then, he discovered that the squealing wasn't coming from there, either.

So, back out of the apartment and out to the broom closet that was between the bone chamber and the women's bathroom. *Now, if I could break into the apartment, then surely I can break into the broom closet, too.* And then he noticed that the broom closet had a steel door. And he wondered, *since when do broom closets have steel doors?*

He went back into the bathroom attendant's apartment now and listened at the wall adjacent to the broom closet. When he placed his ear against the wall, it vibrated so much that his migraine-addled skull got one hell of a massage. And then, Brenner—immediate action.

He didn't have time for the stairs anymore. No, he climbed right up and through the window of the basement apartment and out into the fresh air. And once there, he saw that he'd guessed correctly. The broom closet had a basement window exactly like the bathroom attendant's apartment did.

It struck him just how early the dawn comes at this time of year. Even though it was still completely dark. But already you could feel it, any moment now, dawn would break. Even in the light of day, though, he wouldn't have been able to see anything through the window because it was glued shut from the inside. And state-of-the-art, burglar-proof glass. A one-hundred-fifty-kilo man could take a running leap, and at most, the one-hundred-fifty-kilo man would shatter into a thousand pieces, but the glass still wouldn't budge.

And then Brenner ran over to the Porsche and got the steering-wheel lock. By this point, dawn was so heavily in the air—you could've grabbed hold of it.

And then, as though on command, the birds began to chirp. Brenner couldn't remember a time when he'd ever heard a racket like this. Until the explosion of glass, that is, when he thrashed the wheel lock into the window.

As he climbed down through the window, Brenner could

see less than nothing. But he could feel the dreadful cold of the walk-in freezer. The walls felt icy to the touch, like the igloo he'd built a hundred years ago. And then he found the light switch. And then: good night.

He recognized Löschenkohl's daughter-in-law right away. She still bore a strong resemblance to her sister. Even though only half of her was there. It was only on closer inspection that he was able to recognize Art Collector Marko, even though he was completely unscathed, lying there in his refrigerator case. Brenner had really only seen him briefly that once, though, when he'd said to Brenner at the gallery in Graz: "I pray you're right. But I'd wager you're wrong."

That was two days ago. But it seemed like a different life to Brenner now. And needless to say, it really was a different life for Art Collector Marko.

And then Brenner discovered a third corpse. It was lying on its stomach, but in spite of this, very simple identification. Because Ortovic didn't have any head on. And a moment later, Brenner could feel the steel door opening behind him.

Old man Löschenkohl was wearing the elegant burgundy pajamas that his daughter-in-law had given him on his sixty-fifth birthday. He took just one, two steps toward Brenner and asked him what it was that he was looking for here.

But Brenner couldn't muster a word. Maybe you're familiar with those meat cleavers that you only have to sidle up to a pig with and it splits in two. Well, old man Löschenkohl was trying to sidle up to Brenner a little now.

And how should I put it—he succeeded. Brenner hopped aside so nimbly that I have to say, at forty-five, an accomplishment. These days, though, if you find yourself faced with the choice—off with the head or quick leap—then you take the quick leap, forty-five or not.

But maybe you don't do it quite as nimbly as someone younger might. And that turned out to be why Brenner didn't pull his left hand away fast enough. The cleaver came crashing down onto the butcher block, right where Brenner's left hand pushed off from as he took his life-saving leap. Talk about luck—the old man only hacked off a pinky finger.

Hurt, it did not, but needless to say, no pleasure, either. And on top of it all, Brenner was now stuck in the corner. And it's so easy to say, backed into a corner, figure of speech, but when you're actually backed into a corner, it's something else altogether. The old man was standing—meat cleaver in hand—between Brenner and the door. And the small window hatch: six feet high. Brenner was, in fact, twenty years younger than old man Löschenkohl. It goes without saying, though, when there's a meat cleaver in somebody's hand, age is relative.

And the old man raised the meat cleaver up over his head again. In this instant, and for the second time this morning, Brenner was struck by how unbearably loudly the birds were singing outside.

Because nowadays, when your life is coming to a close, it's the insignificant details that catch your attention. And while the meat cleaver was diving down toward his square skull, Brenner was distinguishing between the good-morning songs of the wagtail, nuthatch, and warbler. Because Brenner had a grade school teacher back in Puntigam who taught them to differentiate between the various birdsongs, and this was what came to mind now as old man Löschenkohl was thrashing the meat cleaver down upon him.

But Brenner heaved himself out of the way again. Although it begs asking here: what sort of sense does that make? Whether he splits you on the second or the third attempt makes no real difference. But in a moment like this, of course, it's purely the instincts reacting.

The cleaver sank so deeply into the butcher block that the old man almost couldn't get it back out. In retrospect, it's easy to say, those two seconds that it took the old man to get the cleaver out of the butcher block, that was Brenner's chance, when he should have overpowered him. But when you're lying in a walk-in freezer with only nine fingers, well, the matter looks a bit different. That's the only way I can explain it: Brenner's just lying there on his chopping block, and his mind's somewhere else entirely.

Not what you're thinking, though, life flashing before his eyes. Because that's what it always seems to mean when you're looking death in the eye, your whole life quickly replays itself in a second: kindergarten, school, driver's license, the gradual dulling of your mind—all of it in one to two seconds like in a movie. But none of that, I'm telling you, was what was flashing in front of Brenner's eyes in those two seconds before Löschenkohl had the cleaver back up in the air again.

Because as soon as a person's closed the curtains on his life, he often gets a little wiser and more relaxed than in all the years he spent desperately clinging to his chunk of a life. And it was in this state that Brenner started connecting the dots in a way that he definitely wouldn't have been able to in all those years of desperation.

A wonderful feeling actually, I've got to say, when a terribly complicated mess solves itself all of a sudden. For Brenner, it was truly uplifting to understand it all so effortlessly in this relaxed state. Where normally a person would make too much of an effort, and precisely because of that, not understand.

In the two seconds that it took the old man to tear the cleaver out of the butcher block, what Helene Jurasic had told Brenner a few hours ago went running through his head again. That old man Löschenkohl didn't demand any real service in return for his millions. Brenner could hear her voice so clearly now that you might've thought she was looking down from the smashed-in window and telling him the whole story again from up there.

How old man Löschenkohl would often come to her several times a week. And how he never asked anything of her. Except that she kneel before him and eat a bank roll of thousands. And how Helene Jurasic, in not even one year, had devoured Löschenkohl's entire fortune. It was all going through Brenner's head again now, while the old man struggled to pull his cleaver out of the butcher block.

Brenner understood now, too, that it had been Horvath's lifelong dream to return as an ordinary waitress to East Styria. And these days, when your lifelong dream's at stake, then you don't just give up on it because of some slimy soldier recruiter. Besides, Horvath could understand why his boss, who'd got sent off to war himself at the age of sixteen, would make mincemeat out of the recruiter. And it was all just an unconfirmed suspicion anyway. And so, Horvath simply didn't want to know for certain, and after that initial suspicion, never tried the fried pieces of meat again, but from that point on, sustained himself only on frankfurters. This, too, was going through Brenner's head, as the old man gripped the front of the cleaver blade with his left hand so that it'd be easier to pull it out of the butcher block.

In his relaxed state, it became clear to Brenner, too, that from the very beginning it hadn't been the bone-grinder squealing beneath his window, but the walk-in freezer. And clear why Löschenkohl's daughter-in-law had disappeared the very day she called Brenner. And that she'd had to die because she suspected something. A correct suspicion, alas. This is what was running through Brenner's head—instead of his life flashing before his eyes—in those two seconds that he still had before Löschenkohl yanked the cleaver out of the butcher block.

Because it simply wasn't true that the recruiter—who'd been given his walking papers so zealously by the old man six months ago—never showed up at Löschenkohl's again. He just wasn't recognizable anymore by the time the health inspectors picked him out of the bone-grinder. And when Rubber Manufacturer Marko was screaming at the waitress that he knew whose bones they were, old man Löschenkohl had to act fast, of course. Because Marko was a war profiteer himself, and he knew for a fact that the army recruiter had disappeared overnight.

Interesting, though, that a murderer can make so many mistakes, and nevertheless, can go uncaught for so long—this, too, was running through Brenner's head now. Because he didn't dispose of the recruiter's bones very carefully. And then he wasn't very successful with his daughter-in-law after she'd ordered the detective to his house.

And when he carved up Blackmailer Ortovic, he thought that, by depositing the head at the soccer club, he could shift suspicion onto Milovanovic, who'd just disappeared, but he failed to reckon with Milovanovic. This, too, was still racing through Brenner's head in the seconds before the old man finally tore the cleaver out of the block and raised it up over his head again.

Interesting, though! His headache had magically disappeared now that the old man was two feet away and aiming right for his skull.

And you see, that's why I always say, you should never give up hope in this life. Old saying, just when you think it can't get any worse, a beam of light—the light-beam's only meant symbolically, though. Because in Brenner's case, a beam of light would've been all wrong. Because a beam of light would've just presented Brenner's head on a platter to old man Löschenkohl. And this, now, really interesting: the beam of light of hope for Brenner was that somebody had turned off the light in the freezer.

"Put the cleaver down, Father."

Brenner could barely see Löschenkohl junior in the darkness. But he recognized his voice right away.

"And come out now," Paul said to his father.

The old man listened to his son without protest. Paul turned the light back on now and asked Brenner, "Are you missing anything?"

"My finger."

"That can be sewed back on," Paul said. "I'll call an ambulance."

"Where exactly did you come from?" Brenner asked.

"From Little Joe's. I wanted to pick up my car."

"If you want to loan me your car one more time, I won't be needing an ambulance."

"The way I see it," Paul said. And then he must have gone into shock, because in one glance, he took in his dead wife and the two other bodies in the freezer as if they were perfectly normal chicken and pig carcasses. And then he went upstairs with his father.

"Or you can call me an ambulance," Brenner said.

"It's fine," Paul said. He looked as if he'd grown up overnight.

And Brenner, too, very calm, as if this wasn't about his own finger at all. And to him, it really wasn't about his finger, because he said to Paul now: "Do you know Manufacturer Marko, the art collector?"

"Yeah, him there by my wife."

"Do you know where he lives?"

"Lived. In St. Martin. The old farmhouse on the edge of town."

"Exactly. Send my ambulance there."

"Why not here?"

But Brenner was already hurrying past Paul and his father, with his finger in one hand and the keys to the Porsche in the other. He ran quickly into the kitchen and bundled his finger in the plastic wrap that's normally used for freeze-packing meat.

Then he got a few ice cubes out of the refrigerator, and put the ice cubes into a bag together with his shrink-wrapped finger. Because first aid, needless to say, always a class about that on the force, and so Brenner knew exactly what he had to do to keep his finger fresh so that it could be sewed back on later.

Then he was in the Porsche, and the steering wheel—instantly smeared with blood, of course, but what can you do.

When Brenner got to the intersection, he could already see a blue flashing light approaching from the left. He waited until the ambulance that was racing up from Radkersburg had passed him, and then he followed it.

Now, maybe it was because of his injury or because the ambulance was already driving so fast, but it was only by the skin of the Porsche's teeth that Brenner could keep up with the ambulance. He was surprised that the ambulance drove with its blue flashing lights on the whole time because there wasn't another car near or far, and so the blue flashing lights really weren't necessary. Needless to say, the volunteers get a kick out of being able to follow emergency response protocol.

And then, they even turned on the sirens. At four-thirty in the morning! But Brenner didn't have time to worry about disrupting Styria's sleep. Because the ambulance was accelerating now. He didn't let it shake him off, though. No, a certain ambition awoke in him, and he thought, *I'm not placing myself in the hands of a couple of Radkersburg volunteers.*

Then, the signs for St. Martin—speed limit through town's fifty, but the ambulance and Brenner blew through St. Martin at one-hundred-fifty. And then, finally, at the very edge of town, Rubber Manufacturer Marko's farmhouse.

And then, the ambulance stopped, and then, Brenner stopped, and then, the ambulance doors sprang open, left and right at the same time, and two people in uniforms hopped out—you would've thought they were riot police.

And then a thunderstorm, just awful, or, to be more specific, it went down like this: when the ambulance driver jumped out of his vehicle, he seemed familiar to Brenner right away. And no wonder, because it was Franz Tecka, the middle-striker on FC Klöch. A bolt of a man, nearly as tall as old man Löschenkohl, nearly as wide as Brenner. His father was a carpenter's assistant, his grandfather was a carpenter's assistant, and his great-grandfather was a carpenter's assistant. And what was Franz Tecka? Secretary at a warehouse.

Because, his father said, my boy should have it better, so Franz went to business school, and now, a job sitting at a computer. Energy like a steer, but all day long, only moves his fingers, so where does the energy go?

Usually soccer practice is good for that, but, in the game against Oberwart, Franz pulled the ligaments in his left knee. Now he just types all day—and no practice at night.

I'm only telling you this so that you might have a slightly better understanding of why Franz Tecka hopped out of the ambulance and rushed the Porsche like a madman and tore open the door.

Instead of screaming his head off, though, he was completely quiet. And maybe that was what Franz Tecka's father always meant when he talked about felling trees. At the last moment before a tree falls over, total silence. Tecka was that quiet now—you could even hear the soft smack of his jaw when it dropped in surprise.

Because sitting in the Porsche was not Porsche Pauli, who'd just made the phone call. And whose face he wanted to scream into that it was strictly forbidden to drive behind an emergency vehicle, and where'd he get his driver's license—a lottery? No, seated behind the blood-smeared steering wheel was the man with the hacked-off finger, who Paul had told him about on the phone. And Franz Tecka was wondering right about now, *why was I driving like the devil from Radkersburg to St. Martin when the injured man was right behind me?*

Needless to say, colossal misunderstanding. In a few words, Brenner explained to Tecka that he didn't call the ambulance for himself but for the half-starved man in Manufacturer Marko's farmhouse. But, naturally, the farmhouse was locked, and Brenner told Tecka he should kindly break into it.

But Tecka's crew member, Paramedic Laireiter, was protesting now. Laireiter was actually the boss of the two of them, and quite correctly, he said, "Breaking down doors is out of the question. We're not permitted to. It'd make us look bad legally."

"Would you prefer to let the man inside starve?" Brenner shouted.

"How do you even know someone's in there?" Laireiter said.

Brenner could tell right away that there was nothing to be done about Laireiter. With a stickler like him you could argue till the Second Coming. And on top of it all, Brenner felt like he couldn't hold out much longer. Because, unbelievable, how much blood you can lose over a pinky finger. That's why he turned back to Tecka now, "If you kick in the door right now, you can save a man's life."

But Laireiter immediately poked his nose back in: "We have to get the police. And then, the police will get the fire department. And the fire department will break down the door."

But Brenner paid Laireiter no heed. He could tell that Tecka was itching to kick in a door, because his right foot was healthy, and in this day and age, the opportunity to break down a door just doesn't come along every day.

"And if Marko turns himself in to me?" Tecka says.

"Marko can't turn himself in to you, because he's dead."

"Who's inside, then?"

"You're about to find out. But if you don't do it fast, it'll be a dead body that you find."

This was the day that Kindergarten Teacher Edith was startled awake at 4:44. Even though she usually slept especially well when she spent the night at Palfinger's. But when she saw all the fours lit up on the clock radio, she thought: *so many fours, and I was probably only dreaming that a grenade just went off in front of the house.*

That was no grenade, though, just Franz Tecka's foot, which, with a single kick, blew open the wooden door to Marko's farmhouse.

Then, what else? Into the farmhouse, Brenner first, and Tecka behind him, and then, after heavy protest, Paramedic Laireiter. But no injured person in the kitchen, nor in the bedroom or the bathroom, and not upstairs, either.

"This is going to be awkward," Laireiter kept saying, half-gloating, half-worried. "This is going to be awkward. You're going to be waiting a pretty long time before you make rank."

"To hell with it," Tecka said, because he was supposed to earn the second point of his blue star on his uniform this summer, but it didn't matter one bit to him now. Because kicking down doors was a feeling that no Star of Life can give you. But a person like Laireiter will never understand something like this.

And now Brenner comes over to Tecka and says, "I can't find the key to the basement door."

A moment later, Tecka had the basement door kicked down.

And it was in the basement that they found him. Nothing

but bones, and no sound coming from him, either. Tecka bent down and took his arm. Tecka's thumb was almost as thick as Jacky's forearm. It wouldn't have surprised Brenner if there'd been a third crack, and Jacky's arm snapped right in the plump hand of the Red Cross.

But Brenner wasn't being fair to Tecka. Because, maybe a brute otherwise, but when it came to taking a pulse, he was delicacy *par excellence*. And he felt very carefully now for whether there was anything still stirring in Jacky.

And then, there was another crash after all. And Brenner was surprised that Laireiter was now suddenly making himself important again, by talking in an insistent tone of voice to the unconscious man.

Brenner didn't understand, though, that the unconscious man wasn't Jacky. And how was he supposed to understand. After all, he was the one who, in the next few minutes while under Laireiter's care, would nearly die.

CHAPTER 13

When Brenner returned to consciousness, he thought only two minutes had passed. And not two weeks, during which time his finger had grown back quite nicely. But, no wonder, he thought he was still in Marko's basement.

"First you save my life, and then you leave me to die of boredom." Brenner had no sooner opened his eyes than Jacky started in from his neighboring bed.

Because Jacky was doing magnificently again. They'd already fattened him up, two whole kilos, all of it by infusion, of course, but as of yesterday, he was even able to help himself to a little bit of mashed potatoes.

Brenner tried to say something, but his mouth still felt a little strange, and involuntarily he thought of Milovanovic, how they had to put a silver plate in his head after Ortovic crushed his face.

When he saw the thick bandage around his pinky finger, everything came back to him—and the memory of it nearly drove him back into a coma. No dice, though, stayed right where he was, because Jacky had been waiting for this moment for days: "You don't need to worry about your finger. They have a specialist here in Graz, Dr. Schneider. He could even sew your head back on if he had to."

"Then Ortovic must be doing better, too," is the first thing that Brenner said after more than ten days of unconsciousness. Jacky actually got goosebumps when, slow and wobbly, his lifesaver squeezed out this remark. Like the heavyweight boxer who always danced so elegantly in the ring that no opponent could catch him. But then Parkinson did catch him. He was no boxer, but this disease where you can't stop with the elegant dancing.

And difficulty speaking's typical with Parkinson's, too, which is why a person might seem a little crazy, but mentally they're completely there. And Brenner was a little tired in the mouth now, too, but mentally, almost quicker than usual: "Who did the police arrest?"

"Old man Löschenkohl's facing all four murder charges: his daughter-in-law, Ortovic, Baumann—"

"Baumann?"

"He was the first. I saw it with my own eyes how he recruited the soldiers."

"It must have reminded the old man of when he was a boy in the war."

"Exactly. And then Marko, that son of a bitch."

"Marko never came back to let you out."

"I don't feel sorry for him. He did business with Baumann, too."

"Where do you know all this from?"

"Says so in the newspaper."

"And what about Milovanovic?"

"Get a load of this, he lives with Jurasic now. All of them under one roof, the Yugos."

One thing that's really interesting. When you've been lying in a coma for a long time, then you don't wake up everywhere at the same time. No, one thing at a time. And almost every part of Brenner was awake now, but his morale—still in a bit of a coma. Because he couldn't have cared less whether they'd actually picked up Milovanovic and Jurasic. Only thing he was interested in was whether Kaspar Krennek had gotten wise to them, in other words, ambition reawakened: "Are the police content with just old man Löschenkohl?"

At that moment, though, Jacky thought Brenner was still halfway in a coma and talking garbled nonsense. And then the doctors stormed in, and in the days that followed, so much happened that Jacky completely forgot what Brenner had said just then.

Horvath came to visit them once. He wanted to give the art another go now, because normal life had gotten to be too abnormal for him. And Paul Löschenkohl visited them once, too. He wanted to give the Grill another try.

Needless to say, difficult, because his father had in fact turned many of his regulars into unwitting cannibals. Great outrage from the people, of course. Three I know personally, they even became vegetarians: a woman from St. Anna, then the elementary school teacher in Klöch, and then a carpenter from Gnieberg. But going without meat made him so agitated that it only lasted a week.

And that was what Löschenkohl junior had been hoping for, too. People forget quickly. Hunger returns, and if you offer them a good price, then they won't stay away for long.

"I freely admit I can't be as cheap as my father."

"How is your father?"

"Not too bad," Paul said. "He's treated decently in prison and is allowed to help in the kitchen a bit. The butcher block I

gave to Horvath," Paul said, changing the subject. Because he
didn't want to talk about his father anymore now. He was still
as transformed as he'd been that night when he'd prevented his
father from breading and frying Brenner. Really not an unlik-
able person, got to admit. Brenner could almost understand
how the shoe seller's sister might've married him.

As Paul was about to be on his way, Brenner quickly added,
"You saved my life."

"Mine, too."

And somehow Paul wasn't completely wrong about that.
My wish for him, anyway, is that he'll be able to manage with
the Grill, because then he would have a job, and a person needs
a job these days, any job, especially when he's as unstable as
Löschenkohl junior.

There are also situations, though, where it's better for you
not to have a job. Where you need nothing but rest and more
rest. For instance, because your finger just got chopped off and
sewn back on again.

But Brenner wasn't getting very far with resting. Someone
was constantly wanting to know something about something,
and needless to say, Kaspar Krennek didn't wait very long, either. He brought Brenner some of those good Belgian pralines,
and within a minute of his arrival, he'd said three times: "I can't
begrudge you any congratulations." It goes without saying, you
only say a thing like that when envy is practically tearing you
apart.

Kaspar Krennek didn't mention Milovanovic again. He
was only interested in how Brenner could have known that
Jacky was in Marko's basement. Needless to say, embarrassing
situation for Jacky now. He looked over nervously at Brenner

to see whether he was going to let the truth slip. That Jacky was Horvath's drug dealer and that he'd blackmailed Marko. But then, a great relief when Brenner said:

"When I was in the freezer, I saw that the daughter-in-law was there, Ortovic was there, Marko was there—but Jacky wasn't there. And I knew from Horvath that Jacky had recognized him for who he was. Marko had gone there to try to silence Horvath. But that only made sense if he'd silenced Jacky first."

"You've got this Super Brain here to thank for your life," Kaspar Krennek said, giving Jacky a bit of a pained smile.

"It's really not all that much of an achievement," Brenner said, refusing to concede.

"Because you can't forget: my life was completely done for there in the freezer. I was missing a finger, and the blood was shooting out of my finger-stump like a jet of water. I don't know if you've ever experienced anything like this, but it's a powerful shock. And it was only because of the shock-power that I figured it out, not because of any normal power."

Kaspar Krennek was getting a little fidgety now, because Brenner was trying to outdo him even at modesty. "Well, anyway, once again, I don't begrudge you any congratulations," he said in farewell.

Once Kaspar Krennek was out the door, Brenner and Jacky didn't waste any time in opening up the Belgian pralines. But Brenner nearly came unstuck with the very first one. Because it was now of all times that Jacky remembered what Brenner had said the day he woke up.

"Why was it, exactly, that the moment you woke up, you asked about Milovanovic?"

Brenner gagged on his white chocolate snail for a second before it slid down his gullet whole.

"And what exactly was Milovanovic looking for at Jurasic's?"

"The Yugos all know each other," Brenner said, smacking his lips.

"But why did you ask about Milo the moment you came to?"

"What are you, a toddler who just learned how to ask a question?"

"What exactly did you find out from Milovanovic and Jurasic?"

You can't escape your roommate in a hospital, though, and Brenner thought, *why shouldn't I tell him? Jacky's been through enough as it is.*

"I'll tell you," Brenner said. But then he sucked on his Belgian chocolate snail for several minutes until it was completely gone before he finally got to talking.

"Pay attention. Ortovic was the striker who, back in Yugoslavia, bashed in Goalie Milovanovic's face. And that was no oversight, no, family matter. Because Milovanovic had a little sister: Jurasic, Helene. Jurasic, because when she was eighteen she got married—nineteen, gets divorced, keeps the name. Then she starts running around with Ortovic. He's got a terrible reputation, so now her brother's got something against the relationship. Ortovic responds in his own way."

Brenner helped himself to another Belgian praline and sucked on it till it was completely gone before going on with the story.

"Then, it wasn't long before Ortovic had Helene out in the street banking for him, and her brother's still trying to get her away from him somehow. Dangerous history, though—not necessarily mafia, but, well, a human life isn't worth much in these circles. When Ortovic goes to Austria with Helene, her brother follows. Because FC Klöch could never afford a goalie that good, silver plate or no silver plate. Doesn't quite add up, though, when he's playing for two thousand schillings flat.

Another Belgian praline now. But even more than the white chocolate, Brenner enjoyed Jacky's impatience.

"These days if a person doesn't know your language, you automatically think that he's a little slow. Milovanovic, though—anything but slow. He found the bones long before the health inspectors did. And he had a suspicion, too, whose bones they were. The exact same suspicion that Löschenkohl's daughter-in-law had later on. Because for the people in-house, it wasn't as difficult to figure out as for an outsider. He didn't tell the police about his suspicion, though. He told his sister about his suspicion. Helene Jurasic."

"Can't you suck and talk at the same time?" Jacky asked, annoyed, when Brenner paused again to reach for another praline. But it was no use, people in hospitals get a little strange, and Brenner was going to enjoy his praline in his own sweet time before he continued with his story.

"When Helene found out, needless to say, she became afraid of old man Löschenkohl and disappeared with the money to Vienna. Because Helene wasn't stupid. Of course, she never told Ortovic about the kind of outrageous sums she swallowed. The whole thing about the money-eating she withheld from him. All Ortovic knew was that Löschenkohl was a perverse customer who left Helene with a lot of money."

"Perverse is good."

"Naturally, though, Ortovic wasn't about to let himself get shaken off. He followed Helene and tried to force her back out onto the track. But Helene gave him a much better idea. She set Ortovic up to believe he could get all of Löschenkohl's money in one fell swoop. As gag money. She didn't tell Ortovic anything more than that. Just gag money."

"And Ortovic thought: gag money for the perverse stuff. But Löschenkohl understood: gag money for Baumann's bones. Basically a misunderstanding!" Jacky laughed.

"Because while Ortovic was on his way down there, Milovanovic called Löschenkohl and pretended to be Ortovic. And explicitly demanded the gag money for Baumann."

"Then, Löschenkohl had to silence Ortovic."

The Belgian pralines were all gone now, and Brenner wasn't feeling so well.

"But why would Jurasic and Milovanovic tell you?"

"They didn't even tell me half of it. But the other half's in the newspaper: old man Löschenkohl's testimony that Ortovic called him and threatened him about Baumann. Even though Ortovic couldn't have even known. All you have to do is put two and two together."

"But why didn't you tell the police?" Jacky asked. Although, secretly, he was glad, because he and Milo had always gotten along well. On the other hand, the two siblings serving up Ortovic ice-cold like that to old man Löschenkohl—not exactly cricket, either.

"Krennek didn't even ask me about it," Brenner said. And in the silence that followed, he thought to himself, a bit arrogantly: *one has to have a proper command of the method for sounding someone out. It's simply not enough to just not ask follow-up questions.* Because, let's face it: compared to Kaspar Krennek, who was too refined in his questioning, even Jacky with his blunt questions came out ahead.

But it wasn't Jacky's questions that irritated Brenner the most, not by a long shot. Most irritating was definitely the head doctor, Frau Dr. Plasser. Because she worked on another floor, but she was obviously trying to reconcile with Jacky now.

Brenner found her visits so obtrusive that he pretended to be asleep. And I have to say, I'm certainly no prude, but that a head doctor would do something like that with a patient when someone's lying in the next bed over, it's just not right.

But please, that's not what we're talking about. Brenner didn't waste his breath over it, either, even though it was happening more and more frequently. Brenner just quietly thought, *as soon as Jacky's healthy again, this romance will be over.*

But a person can be mistaken. Because a month later, Jacky was already Herr Doctor, the honors conferred at City Hall, and Brenner had to serve as his best man. And it wasn't long before Jacky proved to be one of the best hosts that Graz society had ever seen, and his photo always in the gossip papers right next to Caroline of Monaco.

And watch what I'm telling you: people should talk quietly, cocaine or no cocaine. I say, it's not just the cocaine that makes Jacky so popular with the better folk of Graz. No, in the end, it's still because Jacky just has a nice way about him.

But liking a sharp, affable person and having to share a room with him for a week are two completely different things. Now, Brenner had been longing for the day when he'd be released from the hospital. He was just glad he'd finally be able to sleep alone again. And you see, that's why I always say, you shouldn't be glad too soon.

When he was packing up his things, he came across the Vienna phone number that the waitress had written down for him. The number that he'd been thinking was Helene Jurasic's the whole time. But then she told him that she'd never once called Löschenkohl's.

So Brenner thought, *I'll give it a try here from the hospital before I go*. Because it had him intrigued, whose number could it be. But he dialed the first few digits and got an intercept message. Second try, same thing.

"Not home, eh?" Jacky grinned over from his bed, because he had to stay a few more days.

"Wrong number."

"The number you have dialed is not in service," Jacky laughed.

Brenner was thinking Jacky's success with the head doctor was starting to go to his head a little. Honestly, though, I can understand it. Nowadays, when you rise from being the son of a bathroom attendant to the future husband of the head doctor, it takes a little while to fully digest.

But Jacky wasn't giving up now. And you see, it was good that Brenner had told him every little detail. Even the bit about the waitress at Löschenkohl's taking down a phone number for him.

"Let me see that number," Jacky said and reached for the piece of paper on the nightstand. "Is this your handwriting?"

"No, the waitress's."

"Horvath?"

"Exactly."

"That's not the Vienna area code."

"But it says 'Vienna.'"

"No, it says 'Viennese.'"

"Exactly, it says 'Viennese.'"

Brenner had everything packed, and he was about ready to be on his way now. And anyway, the number just didn't interest him. But Jacky had to play the detective. He went looking for something in the drawer of his nightstand, and then he pulled out the folded-up obituary for Löschenkohl's daughter-in-law that his mother had brought him.

"Take a look at this," Jacky said.

And while Brenner was reading "…we announce with deep sadness that Angelika Löschenkohl, born in Vienna, died suddenly," Jacky had already taken the telephone receiver and dialed the number on the note, without the Vienna area code.

"It's ringing," he said and passed the phone over.

When Brenner left the hospital half an hour later, the shoe seller was standing out in the parking lot in the sunshine. She had sunglasses on and half a kilo of lipstick on her face. Her smile had to have been for him because there was nobody standing behind him.

And what should I say: old man Löschenkohl had had this tragic disability ever since his sixteenth birthday. And Brenner, in the middle of the parking lot, well, the opposite problem now. Utterly embarrassing. And at his age, too. But nothing he could do about it. His knees may have been growing softer with every step. But otherwise—talk about a bone man.

"One of the cleverest—and most thoroughly enjoyable—
mysteries that I've read in a long time." —CARL HIAASEN

WOLF
HAAS

BRENNER
AND GOD

MELVILLE INTERNATIONAL CRIME

Wanting out of stressful detective work, Simon Brenner takes a job
as a chauffeur, shuttling a toddler back and forth on the Autobahn
between her high-powered executive parents. But then the little
girl is kidnapped, and he's back in the game again. Told with sharp-
edged wit, suspense that's even sharper, and one of the most quirky,
hilarious, and compelling narrative voices ever.

978-1-61219-113-3 $14.95 US/$14.95 CAN

M̄ MELVILLE INTERNATIONAL CRIME